TITANIOUS

BOOK ONE : RISE OF THE TITANS

Story by Davis Madole
Cover Illustration by Elden Ardiente

CONTENTS

Special thanks to <u>TEAM TITANIOUS</u>

Ace Marrok - Story Consultant

Andres Perez - Story Consultant

Cidercrow - Conceptual Designer

Cream - Conceptual Designer

George Petrakos - Creature Designer

KūWota2k - Conceptual Designer

Patrick Miura - Character Designer

Steve Thao - Character Designer

and William Kearney - Story Consultant

Without you all, this dream would not have happened.

<u>Inspired by the works of</u>

Go Nagai,

Eiji Tsuburaya,

and Masami Kurumada

For Devon & Mark.

Miles into the earth– deep within the planet's depths, 2,500 years ago– there is a dark abyss of fire and brimstone. Towering structures of granite, pillars of bone, pathways of coal, rivers of flame, seas of magma. All is abandoned, for the subterranean world is inhabited by cursed spirits of creatures of all. Their screams of agony echo from across, drowning in despair. Tartarus, the underworld– where souls come for their judgment.

In the far reaches of the realm, there lies a pit, filled with a verdant ooze that flows in a spiral. Eventually, a colossal, muscular figure begins to crawl its way out of the thick mass, covered in wounds that have been sealed, and are in the process of healing. After the giant frees itself from the bath of slime, he marches toward his black armor that has been resting aside, waiting for its owner to don it once more. The figure then covers himself with the dark plating of this armor, and slowly, places the helmet, covered in charred ebony, sporting two horns that protrude from the front, upon his head. The gargantuan male has kept his eyes at rest– but once the uniform has been fitted to his person, he lifts the covers of his eyes, which unleash a bright, deep red flare, filled with rage, hatred, and a desire to destroy. Ares, the god of war, who had just fallen, losing the war on Olympus, tends to his wounds in the trenches of Tartarus.

Another armored figure, one whose head is in the shape of a skull, shrouded in blue flames, approaches the war god from behind.

"How are you feeling, Ares?" the knight asks so sternly.

The horned god glares to his direction for a brief moment, before beginning to wander. "Why are you here? To console me?"

"This is *my* domain, in case you had forgotten." The skeletal warrior trails.

Ares continues to tread along, entering an amphitheater.

The warrior inquires further. "What are your intentions now?"

"I do not answer to you." the god of war leaves a cold reply. "After you had raised an army of the dead that proved itself ultimately useless?"

"You asked for forces, I simply provided."

"And would a servant of mine be so willing to deliver such a pitiful excuse for troops?"

"If we had known the existence of the Elysium Saber, then–"

Ares swiftly turns back to scold the knight. "If I hear another word about what happened, I will tear off that disgusting head of yours!"

The knight stops in his tracks. "You are welcome to try, but I understand. I am only curious as to what your next step is."

"Oh, trust me, old friend. This is all just a minor setback to me. Even if it takes a thousand years, or even longer than that, I will have another chance at conquest."

"Minor, you say? As far as I can tell, Zeus did very well to make sure that–"

"What did I say?"

"If you wish to reign supreme, I suggest we start with the faults in the operation."

"I am very much aware of what went wrong. I am surrounded by weak and incompetent fools who could not do so much as lead a picnic!" The god of war looks off to the distance of the underworld, watching as souls sweep through the dark sky. "Why does he even bother protecting this world and its people? He will see that it will all be for nothing. Violence is within our nature as living and breathing things, so why suppress it? Why not let things play out as they should if the natural order calls for it?"

The warrior peers downward at a slight angle. "Aptly put… for someone who murdered his wife."

"Your point?" Ares faces him again.

"I know not to answer a question with another question, but why should such a genius tactician such as yourself be concerned with such petty matters? If you want to talk about natural order, allow me to clear things up: Zeus is the ruler of Olympus, you are the god of war. It appears you could use a little more self-reflection than I had thought."

"It must be so easy to be as neutral as you are. No need to pick sides, safely hiding away from shame, and free to judge, no matter the consequences."

"With a soul as dead as mine, can you really blame me?"

"Perhaps you intentionally sabotaged my plans by giving me such poor infantry."

"So I am at fault for your blind arrogance? You are lucky to have made it as far as you have with Kronos and Rheia at your side."

"Yet, here we are. You think your shallow compliments will help your case?"

"What case, exactly? If anything, this is all *your* doing. I am being as reasonable as one could be. If you are willing to wait eons before the next opportunity for world domination, we can proceed with this: leave this place now."

The war god draws a smirk.

"Ares…."

He cackles. "I am not going anywhere."

"But am I not useless? Have you forgotten that I am somehow the reason for your failure? Clearly, you have demonstrated that Tartarus has no worth to you."

"Oh, but did I *really* say that? My apologies, old friend. You are correct in admitting how pathetic you are. And since *I* am the genius tactician here, I have a proposal. The only one who is to leave…" Ares proceeds to aim his index finger at the skeletal warrior. "… is you."

"So, you wish to duel? For total control of Tartarus? How far have you fallen?"

"Not far enough. Because control is not all I seek. Oh, no… I also want the luxury of never having to see your horrid face ever again!"

The god of war quickly draws a dark longsword from the sheath at his hip, and charges at the knight. The knight then removes a large scythe from his back, and clashes it down onto Ares' weapon, catching his advance. He then performs a swift maneuver that swipes the war god's sword outwards, and swings the bladed end of the scythe for an upward slash against Ares. However, the god of war recovers just in time to defend himself, rendering the strike useless. Ares parries himself to get closer to his opponent, and commits to a swing at the knight's torso, but he was quick enough to use the blunt side of his weapon for protection. The warrior jabs the end of his scythe to the ground, and uses the momentum of the force to elevate himself, and kick Ares away with both feet. The horned fighter stumbles backward, as the knight regains his footing and stance, the two squaring off, orbiting each other. Shortly, the two fighters' blades engage in combat once more, slash after slash, swipe after swipe, swing after swing– each attack blocked by the next. It is as if the two are enacting an elaborate song and dance with how their swordsmanship plays off against one another.

Eventually, their blades interlock into a struggle. In a moment's notice, Ares gains enough leverage to raise his opponent's scythe, grip onto its staff with a single hand, pull the knight towards him, and execute a powerful headbutt, discombobulating the target. This blow leaves the warrior collapsing backwards, gripping onto his weapon so desperately, as he attempts to raise himself back to his feet. But, Ares comes closer, knowing full well victory is ripe for the taking. Eagerly, he marches toward the downed fighter, though at the second he is about to drive his longsword towards the back of his enemy, the knight swings his scythe towards the war god's torso, which results in an effective blow, as it glides across his chest, blood spraying from his body. Ares screams in agony, and great disbelief– taking in the fact that a brilliant fighter such as him had willingly let himself open for such a devastating attack. This causes the god of war to release his weapon, as he falls backwards on top of the dead ground beneath him.

The knight then shakes off the headbutt, reorienting himself before making his way towards his opponent, weapon in hand. He looks down upon the war god in both pity and disappointment.

"It appears your time for dominion has passed. But through all of the bloodshed and suffering you have caused to this world, it is only fitting that you see a fate similar to those you have slaughtered."

Ares grunts and grits his teeth, containing the pain with all of his might, as blood now runs from his mouth. He looks at the knight standing above him, as he slowly raises his scythe in the air.

"Goodbye, old friend."

Suddenly, a pair of chains, scorching in embers wrap themselves around the scythe, and pluck it away from the warrior's grasp, leaving him in shock. He turns around to see where his weapon had gone, but before him, a feminine figure, wearing armor of her own, approaches.

"Rheia…? Then that means–"

The knight swivels his head back around, but is immediately met with a blow from a trident to his midsection, wielded by one with a demonic visage.

"Kronos!?"

The trident's strike launches the knight backward a good distance, leaving deep scratches in his body. Upon landing, the warrior struggles to breathe, battling for air, as the wind had been knocked out of him, before managing to regain just enough for a cough to draw breath once more. He looks to the two other warriors who had entered the fight, and faces Ares, who carries himself back up, bracing his wound with one of his hands.

The knight shouts. "You bastard! How could an honorable fighter like yourself stoop to such lows!?"

After calling the war god on his hypocrisy, the chains of Rheia entangled themselves around the warrior's arms, with Kronos wandering behind him. Ares steps forth.

"Because I could care less about such feeble-minded principles, or any of that nonsense. All that matters is that I get what I want, and unlike you, I have the fortitude to do whatever it takes to make sure of it."

Soon, large figures proceed to enter the amphitheater– an accumulative total of ten other creatures of varying forms, from beastly to humanoid, make their presence known. In a short panic, the downed warrior looks to his surroundings, upon the revelation that the twelve Titans now obey the will of the god of war.

"You…" he cries out to Ares once more. "What have you done!?"

"Do not act so surprised. I have merely planted the seeds for my upbringing. And it would only be a matter of time before they blossom in my name."

"Killing me will not change a thing!" The warrior cries. "You are only showing that you are a desperate fool who has gone way over his head!"

"Is that so…?" Ares' focus then shifts to the Titans. "Get this cretin out of my sight– but keep him alive for me… May he enjoy immortality living amongst the rest of the worthless mortals on this Earth…" He forms a devilish smirk toward his enemy. "... Nowhere to go… no one to rule."

The Titans proceed to crowd around the warrior, who attempts to fight back in despair, but to no avail. His cries echo through the underworld.

"Damn you, Ares! You can take my world all you want, but know this… you *will* fail!!!"

The war god turns away, and walks toward what was once the throne of Tartarus' former ruler, for he now takes it for himself. Following Ares is Kronos, wielding his trident. As the war god sits upon his new throne, he and the king of the Titans watch as their former ally is forced away.

"Well done, my lord." Kronos bows to his master. "Are you certain about keeping him alive?"

"Letting him live is a far greater humiliation than death. I want him to see my rise to power from afar, knowing there is not a damn thing he can do about it."

"Very insightful, my liege... May your rise to power be a sufficient one!"

"No need for celebrations now. With Tartarus under my control, I must search for the one who created the Elysium Saber, and exact my revenge."

"You mean Hephaestus, sire?"

"Correct."

"But what about Zeus?"

"Zeus will be the maker of his own downfall. As much as I would love to have the satisfaction of ending him myself, I want to relish in the humility of this eventual irony."

"Perfect, your majesty… But there is one thing I must ask."

"And what would that be?"

"The boy."

"No need to be concerned about the half-breed for now. His time will come."

"Understood." Kronos returns to the other Titans to partake in the exiling of the skeletal warrior.

Ares watches on, clasping his fingers together, pondering.

"I will fail, you say? No need to worry, old friend. After all, I am willing to wait thousands of years if it meant that my reign would prevail."

CHAPTER I: AWAKENING

Deep within the mountainous region of Athen lies a tomb of ancient origin– buried for 2,500 years, yet to be discovered. Inside is a red-headed young man clad in silver, resting, encased, trapped in a giant metallic chamber… Until now.

Darkness– the first thing that greets me. I look around, wondering where I am. As soon as I try to sit up, my muscles tighten me to a stop before I lie back down in the coldness that confines me. One breath... two breaths... I rise again, but I tumble onto my side. My body is deprived of energy. Was I asleep? For how long? My legs... they are numb, yet stiff– they ache at just the slightest motion.

I brace around the interior, pulling myself to the exit, dragging my feet, as if I were on stilts. I manage to get out of the metallic monolith, only to be greeted by more darkness. Wherever I am, stone covers the ground, the walls, and certainly the space above. I use my tired hands to guide me around the cavern, hoping to find a way out. Wherever I am is deep within the Earth. I may be going in circles, because I think I must have felt the same stone far too many times than I would like.

Feeling the walls, I navigate my way back to where I had risen. Once I climbed inside, I began searching for a lever. Searching... searching... There. I grasped onto the handle, and proceeded to pull towards my chest. Streaks of lavender and gold emit from this behemoth. I make my leave, and search again for a way out of the Earth, but my legs are starting to fail me... I must keep going.

Thankfully, as soon as the glow begins to fade during my supported march, another one appears. The sun beams into the tunnel, almost making it hard to see, despite having such a prominent presence– but to see what is hopefully a blessed sight, I must suffer temporary blindness. I push forward until I reach the edge. Now, the sun shines down upon the Earth as opposed to a narrow cave. Before me is a field of forests, and what looks to be ruins. Yet, beyond that, a world I do not know. But what I do know is I must march.

"No, no, come on now!" utters a young man in glasses, 19. "It's already March, and this project has been nothing but trouble!"

Frustrated, he kicks his mechanical creation.

"Ow!", he shouts, grabbing the sneaker on his foot, and fumbling onto the cold, unclean floor of his garage. "Guess I should've got some boots, instead of getting a sketchy engine from a different country…"

He reaches for the manual, and scans his eyes through the instructions on how to install an engine for an electric motorcycle, pushing his glasses to his face.

"Ooh… I see now." as he raises his head from the book, and fixes his vision onto the engine. "… It's backwards."

Just a few blocks away, a cloaked frail-legged wanderer finds himself in a farmer's market. After being incapacitated for over a millenia, it has left him with not only fatigue, but hunger. A great hunger. He looks around for an unattended vendor, recognizing he does not have any coin on his person. Desperate, he stumbles down the aisle, and falls to the ground beneath him.

"Hey, stranger."

A voice calls to the lonesome visitor, who then looks up to where it came from. Before his bright blue eyes, a rather large, but strong-looking man kneels to him, and holds to him a bag of peaches and water.

"You look like you could use some." he says with a smile.

The wanderer stares blankly at this gesture, propped up onto his hands and knees, before pushing himself up, and swiftly grabbing the bag.

The man chuckles. "Don't worry. It's on the house."

After hearing this declaration, the wanderer bows his head.

"Thank you."

And with a hint of ferocity, he opens the bag, and sinks his teeth into a peach after pulling one out. The kind man rests the water bottle down near him.

It seems the people are kind. These sweet, succulent peaches may not be enough to completely nourish my being, though I am relieved that I have at least found something I can eat.

However, there is an air– one that feels strange… otherworldly… unwelcomed. A light rumble from afar is heard, and the clouds transition to gray. The vendors in the farmer's market take notice, and begin to close everything. Disappointed sighs from idling customers are released, while others collect their purchases and hastily make their leave. The vendor who had come to the visitor looks to the clouds.

"Guess a storm's comin'. If you don't got a place to go, I'll gladly help you out–"

"It's not a storm." the visitor stops the vendor, staring at the bottle of water, observing a subtle vibration within. "The war…" he speaks, before quickly looking at the large vendor. "It has not ended, has it?"

"War?" The vendor is puzzled. "What are you talkin' about–"

The wanderer immediately grabs onto the shirt of the vendor.

"You have to leave. That was not a thunder strike."

Following his plea, the ground begins to shake, and the residents within the farmer's market start to panic. The vibrations go from a mere rumble, to almost an Earth-splitting tremor. And out from the peninsula, the waters begin to warp. A massive dome shape emerges from the sea, only to disperse, as from the ocean emerges a colossal sea creature– one with a massive, muscular build, almost like a strongman, but much more exaggerate in the belly, neck, and shoulders, with the addition of sharp teeth protruding from a thick, gluttonous, gilled maw, as well as black, soulless eyes with white pupils on the sides of his whale-like skull, and sporting blade-like fins on his back and arms, plus a massive tail. Before the city of Athens, standing at a towering 65 meters tall, covered in sapphire scales from head to toe, the Titan of the Sea: Oceanus, who lets out a mighty, Earth-shattering roar, and proceeds to make landfall.

The market-goers look toward the beast, as they flee for shelter, or to evacuate. The sounds of sirens start to echo through the city.

"We gotta go!" shouts the vendor, as he pulls the visitor to his feet, before throwing him over his back, locking him with one arm, and commits to a sprint down the road.

"Wait!" shouts the wanderer. "I have to go back!"

"I'm sorry, kid, but I can't put you at risk."

"Please let me go, I can handle this!"

"There's nothing we can do, but run. I don't know what you got in mind, but there's no way–"

The wanderer raises his arm, and drives his elbow into the middle of the vendor's back, causing him to fall forward, and releasing him from his arm. Afterwards, the wanderer rolls away to a stand, and starts to hobble in the opposite direction. The vendor looks back at him, sighs, and insists upon rushing back to his pursuit of safety.

As the wandering visitor climbs through the crowds of desperate civilians, amongst the screams of fear and despair, there is a scream of a particular urgency.

"Everyone out of the way, I can't stop this thing!"

Suddenly, the trajectory of the crowds become irregular, but almost to a point where a sort of path is opening. The wanderer swiftly ganders behind him, only for the young man in glasses from a few blocks to collide into him with his electric motorcycle.

"Ah! Sorry, sir! I forgot to install the brakes!" the young man cries as the visitor is clinging onto the bike's front.

The visitor locks his eyes at him.

"Take me to the forest."

"T-The forest?" he stutters. "Why, you wanna go trailing during a monster attack!?"

"We have to go to the mountain!"

"Okay, but if I crash this thing into pieces, it's on you, pal!"

The two youngsters, one panicked, the other more calm, his arms wrapped from behind the other, speed into the forest, and up the hills thanks to the tremendous velocity of the electric bike.

"Hold steady." says the wanderer.

"Yeah, what do you think I'm doing!?" shouts the glasses-wearing driver, as he tries to dodge the trees in passing.

After drifting through the forest, the two find themselves driving up the mountain.

"Here!" The redhead shouts as he forcefully steers the bike into the cave he found himself in with the other young man screaming like a girl at the sudden shift in direction.

"What the hell are you doing!?"

"Have faith in me. I beg you not to stop!"

"I already said I couldn't!"

The two travel further into the Earth. Thankfully, as the sunlight fades from within, the luminescence of the red giant guides them. But despite this, they have to avoid pillars of stalagmites at a high speed.

"Hey, buddy, what's with all the lights?"

"You will see soon enough. Keep going."

Suddenly, the bike begins to sway side to side, losing its balance.

"Hey, uh, I don't think I can control it much longer!" warns the concerned driver.

"Indeed. Your wagon is failing."

The driver eyes back at him in confusion. "D-Did you just call this a wagon!?"

"Brace yourself!"

CRASH!

The bike clips one of the protruding stones, launching the two men toward the rose-colored machine as they skid across the cave floor.

"Ugh, great. There goes my project." the man in glasses reminisces on his damaged creation before looking at the cloaked redhead. "You!" he points. "I don't know who you are, or what your business is, but that bike was about half my tuition!"

The cloaked young man pushes himself up onto his knees.

"Carry me..."

The man in glasses snaps.

"No way! I ain't doing you any more favors!"

"To Titanious... Please!"

"Tita-what!?"

"Look behind you."

"..." He slowly turns back, and to his surprise, a colossal machine, standing at 60 meters tall, covered in crimson, laced in gold. The mechanical giant is partially entombed in the stones that lie before him. The man jumps with a squeak to this unbelievable sight. "What the–!? I-Is that a robot!?"

"You must carry me to it. My legs are too weak, and I have to stop that monster."

"Hold on!" the man in glasses jerks back. "Are you this thing's pilot!?"

"Hurry! We are running out of time!" shouts the redhead.

"Okay, okay, sorry!" The geeked up young man rushes to him, and attempts to deadlift him from the ground, and helps drag him to the mech.

"You have to come in with me if you want to remain safe." demands the cloaked man.

"Uhh, yeah, that sounds good!" the other hesitantly abides as the two enter the machine, and into the cockpit.

"Put me in that seat over there." orders the redhead, gesturing his temple in the direction of a pilot's seat.

The man in glasses scutters on over with his body, and places him in the chair surrounded by switches and levers.

"You may want to step away."

Glasses then distances himself from the pilot.

The cloaked young man inhales deeply. And that moment, a fiery orange glow begins to surround the pilot, as if the heatwaves from his very soul are bringing life to the machine. The space surrounding the two men rumbles as the glow slowly fades into nothing as the pilot grabs onto a pair of switches. And all of a sudden… he exhales.

Optics of violet spark from the crimson goliath's tenacious gaze– and before they know it, the robot known as Titanious moves. Using the levers in front of him, the pilot commands the arms of the vermilion knight to break free from its stone prison, and climb out of the mountain. As this is happening, the man in glasses is screaming and tumbling across the chamber until gripping a safety bar near the pilot seat.

After some time, the rose and gold titan tears open the side of the mountain to release itself to the world, as it pulls itself out, then down the slope, towards the city of Athens where the Titan Oceanus is wreaking havoc.

What in Zeus' name has gotten into Oceanus?

"Hey, buddy, you know anything about that kaiju-lookin' thing?"

"It is a Titan. Oceanus no less."

"Wait, so all that stuff about Greek myth wasn't really a myth!?"

"Whatever you might have read, it is all real."

"Well, I didn't read anything about giant robots fighting monsters! Not that I'm complaining." Glasses nervously laughs and abruptly stops. "Wait, how do you know all this anyway!?"

"Because I was there. I do not know how long ago, but I was fighting alongside Zeus and his army when Ares waged war on Olympus."

"All that stuff was like a millenia ago! Are you a time traveler!?"

So THAT is how long it has been!?

"I do not possess that kind of ability. But this machine was given to me by my father."

"Well, I hope he was smart in that decision, 'cause I don't plan on dying before I get my masters!"

"Hold on tight!"

The mechanical humanoid stops at the bottom of the slope before running imperfectly towards the sea Titan, hobbling once in a while, pulling itself forward using the nearby buildings to brace itself– 25 centuries of inactivity have proven to not be so gracious.

During his rampage, Oceanus sniffs the air, sensing the presence of Titanious. The beast stomps around to reorient himself to face the scarlet mech coming towards him. Titanious then comes to a full stop at a distance from the monster.

"Oh man," nervously squeals the man in glasses, watching through the reinforced transparent shielding from Titanious' belly, "it's like tokusatsu come to life!"

The pilot of Titanious toys with the switches, and has the mech assume a fighting position, similar to that of a wrestling stance. Oceanus puts on an intimidation display coupled with a deep roar, saliva dripping from his teeth.

"You know how to fight this thing?" questions the young man in glasses.

"I may have an idea." responds the redheaded pilot.

The bystander's heart sinks. "I don't like the sound of that."

Oceanus commits to a lumbering charge, screaming at the crimson mech. Titanious staggers, pushing its feet into the Earth as a means to propel itself toward the Titan, transitioning to a slow sprint. The two giants are set to collide. Oceanus gathers enough momentum for a leap toward Titanious, raising its right arm clenched into a fist with a fin blade aimed at the vermilion knight.

"There!" shouts the pilot.

Titanious lunges forward to a stop, ducking just enough to evade Oceanus' attack, while performing a sweep. Soon after, the red robot raises its arms above, now hugging the bladed arm of the beast, and uses its momentum against itself, slamming the sea monster's back into the ground. Oceanus releases a heavy grunt, and Titanious, still clinging onto his arm, slides toward the monster, stomping on the beast's face and pushing it down with great force, all while pulling on the creature's arm in hopes for a submission. Little does the pilot of Titanious know, Oceanus does not submit so easily.

So then the beast reaches his free arm toward the mech, and claws at Titanious' left leg, leaving it with visible scratches, but not enough to penetrate its cratonium alloy. Titanious releases its foot from the monster, but this only gives Oceanus an advantage, in which he proceeds to roll over onto the ruby warrior, grabbing it by the neck. Pinning Titanious beneath him, Oceanus yanks his arm free from its metallic grasp, sliding its sword-like fin across its body, marking the robot's torso. The monster begins to drive its arm toward the face of Titanious, only for it to catch the incoming bayoneted fist. Oceanus follows this by opening its maw, and roaring at the machine's face. A high-pitched scream can be heard from within the cockpit of the red giant. If one were to be in the cockpit with the two men, a very faint sound of the soiling of trousers is also present.

Luckily, before the creature could snap its jaws back together, Titanious posts its right leg against his body, slightly pushing it away so he bites at the air instead. Seeing that his head is now open, the scarlet soldier releases its right hand and starts clobbering the beast upside the head multiple times– just enough to disorient it before unleashing a devastating uppercut, which launches Oceanus back away from it.

The sea Titan fumbles around on the ground trying to recollect itself, and Titanious somewhat struggles to stand back up, now with a scraped torso, and a fairly stable left leg.

"Oh man, that was close." Glasses trembles.

"It is not over yet." claims the pilot.

Titanious props itself up with its right leg. However, shortly after, Oceanus lashes back towards the mech, and reaches both arms at its right leg, entrapping it within his clutches.

"Ah, damn–" the duo inside utter.

The beast then pulls away, swinging Titanious up in the air, only to start swinging and carrying it around before completely slamming it onto a nearby building as it shouts from the bowels of his lungs, crumbling it to pieces. Thankfully, Titanious remains in one piece– however, despite cratonium projecting the mech's body from the force of Oceanus' slam, the pilot endures some whiplash, resulting in him being stunned and fatigued. The creature snarls at the fallen mech, and slowly turns away to continue its city-wide tantrum. In the ruins of Athens, Oceanus takes notice of a large man whose leg is caught in debris– it is the vendor from earlier.

"Help! Somebody help!" he cries.

The man's call catches the attention of the gargantuan sea Titan, who crouches down on all fours, and begins to crawl toward him. The man looks back at the monster in horror, his cries become more desperate. Oceanus smells the helpless human from a short distance, and slowly gapes his mouth open, releasing his nasty tongue, too.

"No! No!!!" the vendor shouts.

Suddenly, the monster gasps in surprise as it is pulled backward by Titanious, who is gripping him by the tail. The red giant manages to drag the aquatic beast away from his target as he roars. Clearly aggravated, Oceanus staggers himself on his fours, and uses his tail to whip away Titanious, driving the vermilion knight into different buildings in an attempt to knock him loose. Yet, Titanious stands its ground.

"You may want to brace for this." the pilot warns his passenger.

"I've *been* bracing!" he exclaims.

Squeezing the Titan's tail with both hands, and to the best of its ability, pivots its left leg before swinging the right one around in its direction while pulling the beast. Oceanus' claws are piercing the ground, but the strength of Titanious' pull causes it to budge, and thus the monster's post breaks loose. Shortly after, the ruby warrior begins to swing the monster by his tail, and pushes its feet further into the ground to generate more force, and soon enough, coinciding with the screams of its pilot, Titanious is spinning, holding the tail tight as Oceanus is being swung through the air. Now it has become a Titan-sized hammer throw. With just enough momentum, Titanious releases, tossing the beast into the air, and towards the coast of Athens. However, the robot's footing becomes unstable after exerting so much force, leaving it no choice but to tumble toward the direction of its launch. This move has certainly taken a toll on the machine's physical capabilities. Realizing this, the pilot wastes no time, and immediately pursues the Titan, who lands face first near the coastline, nearly burying his head into the Earth.

Oceanus pulls his head out from the ground and lets out an irritated growl. Stumbling on over comes Titanious, who proceeds to leap on over to the Titan's back, and takes him for a ride. The creature bellows another roar, and desperately tries to pull the mech off as he stands up, clawing at it– yet Titanious is stuck to him like glue.

"Whatever you do, promise me not to faint." the redheaded pilot tells the man in glasses, who appears to have already failed in his request sometime earlier.

The scarlet soldier then grabs onto the Titan's back fin and attempts to pry it off. This causes the beast to scream more violently, going even more berserk. Titanious continues to brace, and eventually tears the fin off of his back– the strength needed to rip away the fin causes Titanious to fall off the monster's back, but thankfully, rolls into its landing. Oceanus begins to sprint towards the red giant, lunging at it, leading with its gaping maw, to which Titanious, in a swift action, ducks down, and catches the beast with both arms, and drives it into the ground before quickly climbing on top of it and uses the back fin blade to swipe across the monster's throat. A black liquid sprays from the Titan's gash and onto the vermilion knight. Titanious sits still before slowly letting the fin drop from its hand. Inside the cockpit, the pilot is panting heavily in exhaustion after such a rush of adrenaline.

"What is happening? Why did the Titan Oceanus attack humanity? What provoked him? What was his goal?"

The redheaded pilot shakes his head and places a hand near his temple.

"Could it be a warning? But why Oceanus? Are the other Titans involved somehow? ... No... There is something bigger. Something tells me this is only the start of it."

"Oh… jeez…" grunts the man in glasses as he slowly stands up, holding his head as he looks around. "Is it over?"

The redhead breathes. "At least for now."

Suddenly, the area within them begins to quake, gradually becoming greater. The pilot intensely looks around.

"Oh no…" cowers Glasses.

A colossal six-headed dragon emerges from the water, and quickly snatches away Titanious and the two men inside, pulling them into the sea.

CHAPTER II: ALLIANCE

Deep within the waters of Greece, the multi-headed monster, known as the Scylla, pulls the weight of the robot Titanious, wrapping its serpentine necks around the metallic warrior, who struggles to break free from its grasp after having to endure a rugged battle with Oceanus.

"I cannot… get… loose!" The cloaked pilot drives the levers with all of his might.

"Well you better do something!" cries the man in glasses as he clings to the pilot seat. "I'm already prepared to die, but I don't want my body to be at the bottom of the ocean!"

"You are not going to die!" shouts the pilot as if a nerve had struck.

"Oh really!? 'Cause by the looks of it, I was dragged inside a giant robot, only to then get nearly torn to shreds by a giant monster, and now we're gonna drown, 'cause of another giant monster!"

"Last I recall, you were excited about the robot."

"Yeah, but I didn't ask to get caught in some kind of kaiju invasion!"

Soon, the Scylla's trajectory goes upward, approaching the surface. Upon exiting the waters, the six-headed behemoth tosses the red goliath onto the shore of an island– Keros Island, to be exact. Shortly after, the creature slithers back into the sea as Titanious lies in the sand.

The two men exit the mech once again with the one in glasses carrying the other on his back before sitting him down onto the sand. The former looks at his surroundings, and then out to the sea.

"Oh great." he remarks. "This is just great. Wonderful. Fantastic, even."

"What makes you suggest that?" questions the pilot.

"Nothing too big, really, just the fact that I'm now stuck on an island, because of you, you son of a bitch!" The man in glasses raises his voice.

"I am a son of no bitch."

The man in glasses charges at the pilot, screaming. "Shut the hell up, you stupid asshole!"

Glasses tries punching the frail-legged pilot, only for him to block the blow with his hand. He tries swinging again, but gets parried away. Many attempts later, to which all incoming punches get evaded through catches and the swiping of hands, the man in glasses grows more frustrated and gives up. He gets off of the pilot and paces around, grabbing his own head.

"Gentlemen."

The two young men look in the direction of where the voice had come from, the pilot slowly pushing himself up. Before them, a bearded, elderly man with flowing, slicked-back hair, draped in ancient robes, and wielding a dual-forked staff. He walks in their direction away from a home.

"Hades..." the pilot speaks.

The man in glasses swiftly turns to him, puzzled.

"It has been a while, has it not, Hestius? I am glad to see that 2,500 years have shown at least some mercy."

Glasses' jaw hangs, looking back and forth between the two.

"I suppose." the pilot named Hestius responds. "But why are you here? Have you summoned me?"

"There is much for you to catch up with, young one."

"Uh..." utters Glasses. "Give me a moment."

The man in glasses leaves the two alone to ponder everything that is going on. Hades gives him a glance, and back to Hestius.

"Who is your friend?"

"Just a mortal, sir. He is just–"

Hades sweeps his legs with his staff, causing him to fall and grunt.

"You speak like you are not one of them."

Hestius stops for a moment, staring at the ground before looking up to him. "Forgive me, Hades."

Hades reaches the butt of his staff to Hestius, who then grabs it, as he helps him back to his feet with it.

"Anyways, he helped me to Titanious. He may be a child, but I owe him a great debt."

"I'm 19, you moron!" shouts the man in glasses from afar, sitting by the sea.

The red headed young man eyes the god of the dead before him.

"But why are you here, Hades?"

"The same reason as you, Hestius… Because Ares had banished us both to this Earth."

"What?" Hestius elevates his brow. "But, you have all of Tartarus at your disposal… How could he have–?"

"Not anymore." Hades interrupts with a sorrowful tone. "When Ares waged war on Olympus, I provided him my services by raising an army of the dead. As you know, whoever lives or dies is none of my concern. But, when Ares lost the war, he placed the blame of his own failure onto myself, and forced me to exile. Thankfully, the Scylla came to my aid in the midst of my isolation. I would much rather experience the freedom that comes with solitude."

He lowers his chin, staring into the ground. "But, now, Ares rules the underworld."

"But why have you summoned me?" questions Hestius.

"Without Tartarus, I am nothing." he raises his head towards him. "And it appears Ares wants to wage another war, but on Earth. The world and mankind alike have grown weak, so it was only a matter of time before he began his conquest. Thankfully, you happened to awaken at the right moment."

"I suppose… but why did you not come for me earlier? Why did I have to sleep for more than a millenia–?"

"Because whoever lives or dies is none of my concern. Long ago, I had already accepted my fate as an exile."

"If Ares is going to wage war again, how come none of the other gods do nothing? Zeus? Poseidon? Why are they not doing anything?"

Hades pauses before he answers regretfully. "The gods… are no more."

Hestius' pupils shrink at this news, stunned.

The god of the dead continues. "Ares may have lost the war… but most of the gods paid the ultimate price.

Fallen at his hand. And all it took was the might of Zeus to put him in his place."

"The gods… fallen… then my father…?"

"Regretfully so, young one… It does pain me to share this news with you."

Hestius lowers his head. "And if it has been 2,500 years, my mother must be gone, too…"

"I am sorry, Hestius."

The redhead slowly clenches his two fists.

"And what about Zeus?"

Hades lets out a sigh. "Zeus… appears to be on his own terms. Unfortunately, he cannot help us."

"I see…" Hestius faces Hades. "Then it looks like we have to fight Ares on our own."

"Not yet."

"Not yet? What are we doing here, then? What is stopping us from fighting!? Why can we not go to Tartarus now—!"

Hades pushes his staff away and delivers a palm strike to Hestius' diaphragm, causing him to gasp for air before the elderly god grabs onto his right arm, and lowers himself to push his right shoulder between his legs, throwing the young redhead over him and onto his back.

"I may be weak, but you still have much to learn, boy." Hades stares him down, twisting his arm by the wrist. "You lack strength. It is a miracle you overcame Oceanus in your condition. And even so, Titanious must be reconditioned before you can fight again."

Hades throws his wrist away and stands. Hestius rolls over to his belly, propping himself up, coughing.

"But that is not to say that I will not train you."

Hestius looks up at him, gasping gently.

"Like your mother and father, from this moment forth, I will be your teacher, Hestius."

"Uh…" the man in glasses inches toward the two as they draw their attention back to him. "Sorry, I'd hate to interrupt, but what you guys are saying is that Ares– the god of war Ares– is trying to take over the world?"

"State your name, child." commands Hades. "What is your business?"

"Right. I never introduced myself." he clears his throat before pushing up his glasses. "My name is Andy. Andy Balaskas. I couldn't help but overhear your conversation, but maybe I could be of service."

"How so?" asks Hades.

"Well, I am a student in mechanical engineering. I dabble in a little bit of robotics, but I should be getting my masters by the end of the semester, so I'd say I'm pretty good." Andy looks and points to Hestius. "As a matter of fact, I can patch and clean up your robot a bit. I mean, ancient Greek engineering, so it can't be anything too complicated, right?" he tilts his head with a shrug. "Also I can help with your legs, which, if you don't mind me asking…" he strokes his chin curiously, looking at Hestius' lower half. "What happened to them?"

"I…" Hestius stops to briefly reminisce. "I crashed."

"In that robot? You were pretty deep in that mountainside… How are you not dead!?"

"I suppose what would normally kill, or at least fatally injure a human, I only endure a fraction of it."

"When demigods have lived long enough, their abilities given to them through their bloodline begin to appear." Hades adds.

"Ah, puberty." Andy affirms. "Didn't think about that… Anyway, I can help you guys where and whenever it's needed."

Hestius and Hades look to one another, and back at Andy.

The young redhead cracks a smile. "Very well." He then pushes himself back onto his feet, and eagerly reaches his hand out to him. "I am eternally grateful for your support Andy of Balaskas."

"Just… Andy… is… fine." he hesitantly grabs his hand before shaking it. "Anyway," Andy shifts his focus to Hades, "you guys know the deal with that giant monster earlier? 'Cause something tells me that there's more of them out there." He looks back to Hestius. "You said that was a Titan, right? As in the 12 Titans?"

"You were taught well, boy." declares Hades. "I cannot say for sure what Ares plans with the Titans, but they have formed an alliance."

"Then our enemy is more powerful than we could have imagined." Hestius pitches in. "But why Oceanus? Why *only* Oceanus if all 12 have pledged their allegiance to Ares?"

"Maybe he was sent for recon?" suggests Andy.

"So you are a strategist, too, it seems." says Hades.

"I've… seen a fair share of super robot anime." Andy scratches the nape of his neck.

"Is that a sort of text? Where can I find one?" asks Hestius.

"Uhh…" Andy pauses. "Nevermind."

"And with Oceanus slain, they will send another to finish his mission." Hades theorizes. "I sense that his wife Tethys may come for revenge."

"Ah, so more sea monsters." remarks Andy. "I wonder what kind of sushi they'd make."

"Then we have to commence training as soon as possible." Hestius states.

"First…" stops Hades. "How about you two make yourselves at home?"

After trekking for a mile, Hades opens the front door to his island home, as the two youngsters enter. Before them, a living room with a television set-up, dark wooden shelves full of books, all next to a marble kitchen.

Hades steps in, closing the door behind them. "Thankfully, you have more than enough to catch you up to the new world, Hestius."

Andy looks around. "Guess if there's anyone with taste, it's a Greek god."

"And the two of you will have chambers upstairs." informs Hades.

"I take it there's a garage?" questions Andy.

"I will make space for your services, young one." Hades replies. "As for you," he looks to Hestius, "we begin training tomorrow at sunrise."

"And I'll work on something for your legs tonight."
Andy says to Hestius "... If I can get a ride back home, real
quick, that is."

"Thank you. Both of you." Hestius nods.

"Well, then." speaks Hades. "It appears we have
formed an alliance of our own. The few against the many."

"And for the fate of all." adds Hestius.

"'Til all are one." Andy remarks.

CHAPTER III: DISTRESS

Olympus was once in a golden age. Peace and tranquility sang through the clouds, and across the far reaches of Greece. But for every force in the universe, there is an equal, and an opposite. Those who stand against the ideas of righteousness are bound to appear– and as a means to prepare for the day war wages between good and evil, the gods would bear and raise children, so that they may fight for the legacy they wish to preserve.

Out in an arena, lines of these warriors, equipped with armor and a pairing of sword and shield for each one, assume defensive positions. These immortal fighters await orders of further instruction for their training, and obey whatever rings into their eardrums. Orbiting around the soldiers is what looks to be a man with a wraithful appearance, covered in black plating. Yet, this is no man, for it is the god of war himself– Ares. And from afar, lying against a pillar on her soft back, giving a glum glance towards the arena in contrast to her pale beauty, is the goddess of love, Aphrodite– wife of Ares. Along with her, a small redheaded child, about age 5, hugging at her leg, and watching the warriors from afar in fascination with their coordination.

Momentarily, a man in silver armor, and fiery hair flowing from his head and face, approaches the goddess and child.

"Hestius, my boy!" shouts Hephaestus, the god of fire and smithing.

The redheaded child swiftly turns to the man with a sudden surge of glee, and runs to the best of his ability towards him. The fire god kneels before the young boy pounces into his embrace. A laugh echoes from the two, and Hephaestus rises, holding his child to his person with a single arm. Aphrodite moves her glance to the father and son, peering through her silk, gold bangs, and lets out a very small, muffled chuckle.

"You have been staying out of trouble, yes?" Hephaestus asks the little one.

Hestius quickly shakes his head in response.

The fire god looks at the love goddess with a minute smile. "Has he been good today?"

"He has." she replies. "Ever since I got him from Gabriella's, he has behaved well. He wanted to see the valley, so I abided by his request."

"Good… Very good." He rubs Hestius' back, walking to stand beside her, facing the arena. Slowly, he forms a sorrowful expression. "It is a shame I am forbidden from seeing her… If only I, myself, could see the impression she leaves on this fine boy."

Aphrodite turns her head to face him. "I know how you feel… I sense it in your heart. I can only imagine the pain it brings."

"It is comical how we are practically invincible, yet nothing protects us from the struggles we place upon ourselves."

"The tragedy of immortality, indeed."

"You know… I still do not blame you after all these years."

"You say that, yet I am still sorry…."

"You are the goddess of love. It is within your nature. You deserve to be happy, even if that happiness is with someone like Ares."

"Yes, but you deserve happiness, too, do you not?"

"Well… not even I am in control of my own destiny, it seems." Hephaestus looks to his child, who is watching the soldiers from a distance. "For now, he is all I have left."

"Gabriella must be teaching him very finely. You two have brought a very bright boy into this world."

Hephaestus nods. "Indeed, we have… And I have no regrets, as long as it means he grows to become a great man."

Aphrodite watches the two, then back at the arena, zeroing in on Ares, who is barking drill orders. "Five years… The truth will come out, eventually. You know that, right?"

"It is inevitable. But regardless, I appreciate you for taking on the role of a surrogate. Even if things between us did not turn out for the best, I still owe you my life, Aphrodite."

Hestius turns to the fire god. "Father?"

"Yes, my boy?"

"Mother says they are… s…s-sull-jers?"

"Indeed, they are, Hestius. They are fighters who will protect our land."

The child looks back at the crowd again with a hint of amazement. "Can I be one?"

Aphrodite releases a soft giggle.

Hephaestus looks at the boy with confusion. Watching as his son looks out into the distance, marveling at the armorclad warriors, the god proceeds to smile, and look in the same direction. "If that is what you want."

Return to now, on Keros Island, as sunbeams rain down upon the beach. The ocean rages on in waves, and gulls soar through the skies. And on the crystal-like shore, Hestius– sporting a compression shirt, athletic shorts, leggings, and new metallic leg braces strapped above and below his knees– holds a squat. His feet spread slightly beyond shoulder-width, his depth being parallel to the Earth beneath him, his arms extended forward, his palms facing the sea, his index and middle fingers reaching the sky, his thumbs bridged together, his core burning, his face dripping in sweat, and his breathing heavy, yet calm.

"Hold still." demands Hades, who hovers around the redheaded youngster.

Hestius responds by inhaling another gust of air through his nose, only to release from his mouth. He then shuts his eyes, as if to distance himself from the tension he endures, slowly bowing his head. Hades then flips his staff around and swings the end of it towards his abdomen, to which Hestius gasps, but still maintains his position. Hade then flicks the staff towards his chin, and knocks it upward.

"Chin up." he commands.

Hestius continues to hold his position, but his body gradually begins to tremble. Hades slowly steps toward him, staring. As Hestius' shaking becomes more rapid,

Hades tosses his staff aside, raises his right foot, and it toward Hestius' left knee. Hestius folds sideways upon impact, but saves himself with his left arm, keeping his right up for balance. Hades advances for a left uppercut, to which Hestius pushes off of his right foot, and deflects his strike with a right elbow, and follows with a left uppercut of his own. However, Hades recovers by catching his incoming fist with his right hand, and raises his arm up, leaving his side open. Hades then swings a left cross through the left side of his abdomen, followed by an elbow towards his back, which causes Hestius to stumble around before eventually maintaining his ground. Hestius flips back around, assuming a wrestler's stance.

"Fix your stance, child." orders Hades before assuming a stance reminiscent of a kickboxer's. "You must learn to adapt in the face of adversity."

Hestius gently nods as he adjusts his stance to match his. The two men shift toward one another to spar, Hestius delivering a jab to Hades' face, to which he weaves away. Hades then commits to a cross that gets swept away by Hestius's right arm as he orbits around him in the opposite direction. As Hestius slides away, Hades sweeps his left leg underneath him, causing Hestius to fall backwards. Hades then follows the redhead to the ground, pinning his knees beside his torso, grabbing his shirt by the neck and proceeds to throw a punch. Hestius crosses his arms in an 'X' formation to defend himself… but Hades has not landed the blow, and remains immobile, looking down at him.

Hestius sighs and removes his guard. "Why can I not train in my wrestling style?"

"Because much like the world, hand to hand combat has evolved. And to be stuck in the old ways, then may you fade with the sands of time itself." Hades replies before standing back up. "Besides, you have already mastered your wrestling technique, despite your clear handicap."

"I suppose." Hestius slowly pushes himself to his feet. "Though I could always go back to it whenever it is necessary."

"You could. But that would make you predictable. The Titans must not know your every move." Hades grabs hold of Hestius' hands. "Today's training is done. While your skills still need work, you are starting to gain your old strength back. Perhaps I should give Andy my thanks. As should you."

Hestius looks down on his hands, and slowly faces him. "Thank you, Hades."

Hestius returns to the beach house, and enters his and Andy's room– Hestius' half being rather bare bones and basic, while Andy's is littered and plastered with posters, comic books, and DVDs of many superheroes and robots– collectible figurines ranging from giant monsters, Tsuburaya's Ultra heroes, Ishinomori characters like the various Super Sentai and Masked Riders, plus a variety of mobile suit model kits (some of which even change into various means of transportation), all inhabiting the shelves.

"Hey, what's up, Hes?" Andy leans his head back, calling to Hestius as he watches a pirated copy of *Shingeki Sentai Titanranger* on a small couch.

Hestius looks at him, confused. "Are you not busy with your studies?"

"Figured I'd take the day off. Chipping away for over a week right after moving in's got me beat. I see your braces are still good?"

"Yes." Hestius plops down onto his bed, sitting. "I believe I have given my thanks already, but I am grateful."

"Eh, don't sweat it. I need to keep myself busy more often."

"Of course." Hestius wipes his brow with a small towel, taking a deep breath before lying down.

"You sure you don't wanna shower, man?" questions Andy. "You're gonna stink up the place."

"I will… " Hestius replies as he relaxes. "Give me a moment."

"You know, when Hades said chambers, I thought he meant plural."

"Do you not have enough space for your belongings?"

"Nah, I do. I mean, last time I had a roommate my freshman year, things were just weird. He wouldn't be back til the middle of the night, and it really wrecked my sleep schedule. Didn't help that he'd come back with a different girl every week, meaning I had to hide my model kits in the drawers."

"This roommate– he sounds undisciplined, and lacks ambition."

"I'd say that's an understatement."

"Tragic."

"Yeah, no kidding."

"Well, Andy, I promise you that I will not follow such an example."

"I'd greatly appreciate that… And by the way, what's that stuff Titanious is made out of? It's not like any metal I've seen."

"Cratonium. It is an element we used in Olympus to forge weapons and armor for war."

"Oh really?"

"The metal is what keeps Titanious durable in battle. Think of it as a shield."

"Makes plenty of sense. I was wondering why I only saw internal damage. Guess that only makes my job easier."

Not long after, Hestius stands in the middle of a bathtub as water showers down on him. Running his hands up his face and through his hair, memories of his mother, father, Olympus, and the old Earth echo in and out of his mind. Despite living in a whole new world for more than a week, he is shackled to the weight of a distant past.

Afterwards, Hestius enters him and Andy's room again, but in a white tee, black sweatpants, and his leg braces, wiping his face and hair with a pink towel.

"Hey now, you haven't been showering with those have you?" Andy gestures to his braces.

"Of course not." Hestius replies.

"Good. Don't want them getting rusted." Andy yawns as he watches more tokusatsu.

Hestius tosses the towel aside, and takes a look at the screen, slightly raising an eyebrow of curiosity. He makes his way towards the couch, and takes a seat beside Andy, staring at the television with him.

"What would you call this type of character?" Hestius asks, pointing to a frame of a silver giant assuming a boxer's stance.

"Oh him? We call them superheroes." Andy responds. "They've become very popular in this day and age."

"Yet they only exist in these images. Their impact must be profound!"

"This guy has been around since the 60's, and they're still making shows about him every year. He's kinda this representation of the human spirit– and how while we're flawed, we can still achieve greatness, and all that stuff."

"That is quite interesting. I can see how humans enjoy these stories."

"Yeah, though not everyone's into it."

The two watch the silver giant on the screen battle a giant creature. Hestius releases a small laugh.

"Funny. This one is kind of like Oceanus."

"Oh yeah?" Andy gives a chuckle. "There might've been some influence. In fact, a lot of heroes, monsters, and stories are modeled after ideas that we've read in folktales, scriptures, and even records of ancient history."

"Tales as old as time… breathed into stories that would become timeless themselves…"

"Exactly, dude… You know, I never thought there was anything like Titanious in your time. Always thought it was just Talos"

"Ah, yes! I know of Talos!" Hestius swifts his head to Andy. "He was created by my father!"

"Wait." Andy squints his eyes to do a double take before widening them, and looks at Hestius. "So Hephaestus is your dad? Like, your *real* dad?"

"Was, but yes. He built Titanious for me to fight for Zeus. In a way, it was a successor to Talos."

"Then that would make Ares–"

"My uncle, yes."

"I had a feeling this involved an estranged family dynamic, somehow."

Hestius gives a slight chuckle. "I suppose it is rather common. Olympus had many complicated relationships."

"No kidding. And my condolences, man."

"Thank you. It is quite a lot to think about, and it has not left my mind as of yet. All I can do is simply persevere in his name– it is what he would want."

"That's good, man."

"So your parents… are they–?"

"They live in America. I'm studying abroad here, so I am quite a ways from home. Got a little sister, too." Andy laughs.

"Well, then. I am sure once you reunite with them, they will marvel at your growth, and be proud of what you have become." Hestius smiles softly.

"Oh, I sure hope so!" Andy laughs again before he grabs his cell phone from the side of him to check through it. Upon scrolling through notifications, his body stiffens.

"Dude…" Andy utters.

Hestius is visibly confused. "What is it?"

Andy turns his phone toward him. On the screen is a news broadcast of a giant frilled and tentacled monolith sprouting from just off the port of Piraeus at 75 meters tall, covered in emerald scales.

"You know anything about this?" Andy asks.

"Tethys…" Hestius replies before looking at Andy. "What is Titanious' current condition?"

"Ready to go when you are."

Hestius is on the move, eventually exiting the island home with Andy following behind, only to see Hades standing on the beach, facing the ocean.

"It appears our prediction was correct." Hades declares. "Tethys has come for revenge."

"Indeed." Hestius approaches Hades. "But, she has not begun any sort of attack... why?"

"The answer is quite simple, boy. She is waiting for you. The Titans know you are here on Earth, and are prepared to face you at any given moment." Hades turns to face Hestius. "But the real question is: are you prepared to face them?"

"At any given moment." says Hestius.

"Go. I shall summon the Scylla to take you to your destination."

Hades faces the ocean, and proceeds to raise his arms in the air, holding his staff in his right hand, and then grips it with both hands before jamming it into the sand beneath him.

"Remember your training." Hades urges Hestius.

Hestius gives a nod and heads for Titanious, climbing into the cockpit before activating it with his spirit. The Scylla slithers ashore, sliding besides the scarlet soldier, ready for it to hitch a ride. Titanious approaches the multi-headed serpent, and helps itself onto its back. Shortly after, the two giants descend into the sea, and embark on their way to Piraeus.

Andy starts to mosey over to Hades. ""So… What should I do?"

Hades looks over to Andy. "I task you with the honor of providing a feast for our warrior's return."

"Oh, uh…" Andy gives a nervous chuckle. "I'm not exactly the cooking type."

"Well then, young engineer." Hades grasps Andy's shoulder. "It looks like I will have a new student."

Andy turns pale. "I guess I could take a break from dealing with engines."

Submerged below the surface, Titanious and the Scylla journey their way through the beautiful blue Sea of Crete, passing through all sorts of sea life. Two find themselves with turtles and plenty of schools of fish. With great focus and intent, Hestius grips the switches in front of his seat.

Off the port of Piraeus stands Tethys in her beauty, nearly resembling a flower. Civilians within the vicinity are out to gander at the creature– some take photos and video of the Titan as several camera crews cover the event. Moments later, the Scylla rises from the waters, and sweeps around the port, Titanious on its back. Onlookers proceed to either flee, or stay behind to witness the act, as if they are being met with a giant-sized gladiator battle that is about to commence. As the Scylla comes to a stop in front of the towering Titan, Titanious climbs down off its back. The Scylla proceeds to make an exit, leaving the two alone, both standing in the middle of the water. The transparent shielding from the crimson knight's belly opens, as Hestius walks to the edge of his cockpit, and calls out to the beast.

"Tethys!" he shouts. "It is I, Hestius– son of Hephaestus!"

The creature grumbles softly, only for it to echo at Hestius' words.

"Listen… I apologize for your husband. And I understand that is why you have come… But, please, tell me. Tell me why Oceanus started attacking humanity!"

Tethys' growling becomes louder.

Hestius grows frustrated at the lack of a response. "What have the Titans planned with Ares!? Tell me, or I will execute you, like I did Oceanus!"

Tethys snaps. An ear-piercing cry is emitted from her being. Slowly, she unravels the tentacles that have hugged around her, revealing an aquatic body of coral, and an empty face that slowly raises, eyes of azure, with an opal frill surrounding the back of her neck. As the tentacles of Tethys splay out, she does the same with her vaguely human-like arms.

"So be it." Hestius returns to the seat of his cockpit, the shield closing itself. The red mechanical giant then assumes a slight wrestling stance, as if to anticipate Tethys' next move.

Tethys sways her tentacles around as Hestius eyes each one of them, tense. The Titan pulls one of her tentacles back, and proceeds to flick it in Titanious' direction. Hestius focuses on the incoming attack, and uses Titanious to duck away from the blow. Shortly after, another tentacle comes swinging in towards its side, and to the best of its ability, the red giant rolls over it, its back only grazing it, causing an imperfect landing on one knee and hand. From above comes another tentacle, coming to slam down onto Titanious, who is quick enough to catch it with both hands. The vermillion knight starts pulling at the tentacle to get closer to its enemy. However, another tentacle comes by, and sweeps Titanious by the feet, knocking it down onto its back before it rolls over to recover. But the strike is followed by another tentacle that grabs the crimson mech by the shin, and pulls it toward the colossal creature. Titanious desperately tries to brace itself by grabbing onto the water's floor, but to no avail. Tethys then swings her tentacle upward, launching the ruby warrior into the air, causing Hestius to shout as he's tossed, and gripping onto the controls for dear life. Before Titanious could descend, Tethys sends another tentacle to then smack the mech into the water. The impact leaves a gigantic splash, and a crater beneath the machine.

Hestius lets out a grunt after enduring the whiplash of the attack as he starts to feel nauseous and disoriented. As the scarlet soldier idles, several tentacles slide over, and wrap themselves around the limbs of the machine, as Tethys summons them to bring Titanious to her. The scaled beast splays out the ruby warrior's limbs, holding it slightly above her. She slowly brings her face closer to the mech, squinting her eyes as if to examine it, letting out an ugly segmented snarl. Retracting her head back, she slowly but surely begins to pull at the arms and legs of Titanious with her tentacles. Inside, Hestius holds his head.

"*I... have to... fight...*" Hestius thinks to himself as his vision crossfades in and out while feeling around the controls and levers.

Tethys' pulling grows stronger.

"*I... cannot...*"

The joints of Titanious gradually become more loose.

"I cannot..." Hestius softly speaks as he slowly regains his vision. Then, he shouts. "... LET YOU WIN!"

And with all of his might, Hestius drives the controls, causing Titanious to forcefully cross its arms to grab the tentacles on the opposite sides of either one. A rageful scream can be heard from within the robot as the machine's grip becomes tighter, its fingers puncturing through the flesh of each tentacle. Suddenly, the Titan lets out what resembles a gasp as the machine's temperature begins to climb. And after what sounds like a thundering cry of strength from Hestius, Titanious manages to tear off two of Tethys' tentacles, causing the monster to screech out in pain. After their removal, the vermilion knight chucks them aside, and attempts to do the same with the tentacles around its legs. Immediately following, Tethys submerges the machine into the water, and begins to retreat towards the ocean, to greater depths, pulling Titanious behind her with more tentacles strangling around the mech. The ruby warrior continues to fight on, pulling and punching at each tentacle with all of its might to break free, almost burning up as its temperature becomes higher and higher. This would leave burn marks on the Titan's tentacles, forcing Tethys to release the crimson goliath, and continue swimming. Titanious is dropped onto the ocean floor, and Tethys shakes and turns her scales to reveal a reflective pigment that renders her invisible to the eye.

Hestius looks through his surroundings, stunned at the sudden disappearance of his opponent. Shortly after, Titanious is blindsided by a flurry of blows from the creature's appendages, launching it to another part of the sea floor. After landing, the mech is met with her tentacles once more, as they twist around it, and slide Titanious across the ground. The red giant hugs its torso around the tentacles, and starts to roll in the opposite direction of his trajectory, resisting Tethys' force. This manages to pull the Titan toward it, additionally slamming it into the ground. Titanious eventually breaks free, and starts to feel and climb its way to Tethys' main body to attack, but is suddenly pushed back with great force, being shot back against a rocky structure. Hestius recollects himself as Tethys is still nowhere to be found. He examines the area around him, but starts to hear very faint swirls and swooshes within the water. After noticing this, Hestius stops, and proceeds to breathe in through his nostrils, and release air from his mouth as he gently shuts his eyes.

"Be one with me, Titanious… Let me feel what you feel… Remember my training."

Hestius remains still, breathing softly. *"If you can hear me, father… guide me to victory."*

Titanious slowly assumes a horse stance– spreading its feet apart beyond shoulder-width, shifting its depth parallel to the ground below, reaching its arms forward, palms facing out, index and middle fingers up, and thumbs bridged together. It remains alone, isolated in the vast bottom of the sea. Hestius feels the cooling embrace of the ocean around him and the vermillion knight, slowly becoming one with it. Soon, a ripple within the water occurs– as if a projectile were rocketing towards the machine's position. At the moment it would strike, Titanious immediately shifts away, causing the blow to miss its head, and crashing into the mountainous structure behind it. Shortly after, another comes from the side, to which Titanious pivots around on his left leg, rendering the attack useless. And another one comes from below, and the ruby warrior posts his right leg outward. The next comes for its right arm, as Titanious swipes it away. Then, its chest, which is met with a parry from its left arm. There it is. Something is coming. It is approaching at a rapid velocity, and the colossal machine stands its ground, waiting for the right moment. Collision is imminent, and the invisible target draws near. However, it is caught with a swift catch from Titanious' right hand, as it begins to squeeze. A compressed yelp escapes from the target. It has become clear that the scarlet soldier has clenched its hand around the neck of Tethys. Hestius slowly opens his eyes, as the optics of Titanious shine in amethyst. The mech hurls the Titan into the structure beside it, and proceeds to pummel away at the beast with its own flurry of furious fists. Tethys cannot and must not escape from it. With each strike, the monster cries out in pain, even reaching the point of bleeding its violet essence, which starts to cloud the waters around the two giants. Titanious presses on, delivering a combination of different jabs, crosses, and hooks, almost coming off like a hunter who had just captured his prey, ready to finish his game. Hestius is completely locked in– focused entirely on destroying Tethys, driving the switches back and forth in varying combos with a raging heartbeat. The Titan's skin becomes visible again, revealing all sorts of bruises as she desperately tries to pry away from the mech– yet her efforts are futile, as the temperature of Titanious starts climbing once more, and even starts burning her.

Gabriel...

Hestius stops, as does Titanious. He swiftly looks around, as if something had called to him. The red headed pilot then takes a moment to stare at the beast, who's wriggling weakly beneath him, letting out a series of small, faded screeches and growls. Suddenly, the lilac blood that shrouds both of them starts to feel warmer, yet Hestius is tense, as Titanious begins to cool. The pilot's heart pounds greater than before, as he breathes heavily, visually examining the condition of Tethys, whose cerulean eyes slowly turn dark. The Titan becomes motionless– her life has escaped her being at last. Hetius feels an unnerving sensation in his hands, as he then shifts his focus on them, watching them tremble. He attempts to grab his wrists to stop it before trapping them beneath either side of his armpits. Suddenly, he himself starts to tremble.

"W-What is this feeling...? I did what needed to be done, but... why am I feeling a pit in my stomach?"

After giving himself time to recover by taking deep breaths, Hestius grabs onto the controls of Titanious. The mech backs away from the Titan's body, facing it. Moments later, the machine approaches the body again, and grasps it with both hands, proceeding to carry it through the ocean floor, walking to an open trench just far off.

Finally, after meeting the edge of a cliff, where darker depths await, the vermilion knight looks down upon the Titan. Shortly after, the vermillion knight releases Tethys' body, and watches as it slowly sinks into the Earth– becoming one with it.

"I could not give your husband a proper burial...
but this is what he would have wanted for you."
Titanious marches back, returning to Keros Island.

CHAPTER IV: SPIRIT

Nighttime arrives. Hestius, Andy, and Hades all commence with dinner at the table. With the help of Hades, Andy had prepared platters of lamb, potatoes, and an assortment of fruits and green vegetables– fit to satiate the strength of a warrior.

"I must say, young engineer." Hades calls to Andy as he chows down on a lamb chop. "You may have another niche."

Andy laughs nervously. "I guess so… Though, how come you don't have any vegetables if you don't mind me asking?"

"It is the souls of the dead that bring me life."

There is a pause amongst them.

"... Not gonna argue with that." says Andy, beginning his meal.

Hades looks across the table. Hestius has his elbows propped onto the table, his hands folded against his forehead, staring down at his plate.

"Hestius." Hades calls.

Hestius raises his head, facing his teacher.

"You must be hungry after fighting, are you not?"

"I should be, yes, but… I do not feel any hunger. My mind is probably just too tired to eat."

Hades eyes him.

"Very well… Though if you wish to train with a lack of energy, that is your choice."

Andy watches Hestius with a hint of concern, but continues to feast. The redheaded pilot looks down upon his food again.

Some time later, Andy and Hestius prepare to rest for the night.

"Hey, are you doing okay, man?" Andy looks over to Hestius.

"Just… fatigued. That is all." he answers.

"Alright. Well, if you need something, don't be afraid to holler."

"Understood." Hestius replies, getting his bed ready. "You rest well. Titanious will need plenty of repairs."

"I'm aware, dude." Andy gives a thumbs-up with a smile. "I'll get it handled."

The two lie under their covers. Andy is fast asleep after taking some melatonin gummies. Meanwhile, Hestius stares up at the ceiling, reminiscing on the battle he had just endured. But not necessarily does he focus on the potential near-death experience, but the aftermath. The dying breaths of Tethys float through his mind, as if to leave a looming imprint. Hestius recalls the undersea burial he had given her– yet, there is still a void in his soul. Only time will tell when this void will shut, as it is a healer of all wounds– but only on its own accord.

Three days later, Hestius and Hades are going through combat training with wooden poles on the beach. The two have engaged in an altercation with their sticks for some time– for every strike, there is a block. However, Hestius grows sluggish in his movements, eventually leaving himself open. Hades proceeds to jab his pole into his chest, followed up by smacking his head with it.

"Focus." Hades commands.

Hestius nods, shaking his head, and swings his pole to the god of the dead's side, only for it to collide with his pole. Hestius' pole is then smacked away, as Hades swings for his side, which crashes into the redhead's ribs. Hades retreats his pole, and posts it into the sand, watching Hestius as he recollects himself, taking deep breaths.

"What is your problem, boy!?" begs Hades. "Ever since you had come back from your battle with Tethys, you have become nothing but sloppy and undisciplined!"

Hestius continues to breathe. "My apologies, Hades… I do not mean–"

"Has the essence of death plagued your mind?" Hades interrupts.

"I… Yes, it appears it has, but… I have not done anything wrong, have I? I killed Oceanus. I killed Tethys. But why do I feel like I *have* done something wrong? I-I did what I was supposed to!"

"Yes. You have." Hades approaches the young fighter. "But you must understand, *warrior*. It is your life, or theirs."

"I understand, but Tethys… she wasn't attacking humanity, or anything."

"But she was out to kill you."

Hestius pauses, looking up at Hades, and then down. "Maybe… I am not fit for this war."

"Boy." Hades replies. "Have you forgotten what you are?"

Hestius fixates back to his master.

"You must remember that what you have is neither an honor, or a curse– nor is it a right. It is a privilege. Are you really going to let all of mankind face punishment, because you reject your privilege? Because if so, tell me… What would become of you?"

"... Forgive me, Hades." Hestius hangs his head slightly, his eyes drifting off to the side. "That was rash of me."

"You yourself once said that you wish to fight alongside the gods. But to know true power, you must be willing to make the hardest decisions." Hades looks to the ocean. "Even if lives are at stake… And it is important that you uphold the very ideals you stand for. Unfortunately, that is the cruel reality of war."

Hestius watches Hades once more.

"Oceanus and Tethys are gone. Their souls now dwell in Tartarus. There is nothing we can do, but keep moving forward." Hades eyes back at Hestius. "Promise me that you will remain strong from here."

"Yes, Hades." Hestius answers.

"Strong enough to carry the weight of more blood on your hands?"

"Of course."

"That you will not falter in your mission?"

"Absolutely."

"And that you will not stop until Ares and his forces are destroyed!?"

"With my entire being!"

"Swear not to me, but on your mother and father that you will remain victorious!"

"I swear on my mother and father that I will win!"

Hades stares down at Hestius. "Very well… Then our training will continue tomorrow."

"Thank you, Hades."

"But I have just one question…"

Hestius eyes his master with curiosity.

"Have you awakened your power yet?"

"My… power?" Hestius ponders for a moment. "No, I do not think I have."

"I sense it may come soon enough. It all depends on the hierarchy of the gods. This is why Hercules was able to use his strength at birth, for he was a direct descendant of Zeus. But, as you are the son of Hephaestus, it may take you a while."

"Right…"

Hades rests a hand on his shoulder. "Yet, you still possess the strength of your mother."

"What do you mean?" Hestius looks on with curiosity.

"Your spirit, young one– it is the same as hers. Even if we lack it physically, wisdom can become our greatest strength. Power without perception is useless, for it would have no true value… Now, go rest. So that you are ready when another Titan arrives."

Later, Hestius goes to check on Titanious while Andy is working on repairs, hanging on a harness attached to a pulley. Sparks fall from the midsection of the crimson goliath, as the sun makes it glow. Andy leans his head down to Hestius' direction.

"Hey there, Hes!" he shouts. "Almost done here."

"Understood!" Hestius shouts back.

"Oh! By the way, I got something for ya. Check that case!"

Hestius then looks at a silver case lying on a beach. He slowly approaches, while Andy finishes up repairs, only to then lower down, and free himself. Walking over to the pilot.

"Go ahead and open it!" urges Andy.

Hestius reaches down, and opens the case. Inside a red and gray form-fitting padded suit with yellow accents. Complete with boots, gauntlets, shoulder pads, and a helmet. Hestius examines the items as if to make sense of their being. There is a sense of familiarity with this suit– likely because Andy modeled it after some of his favorite tokusatsu heroes.

"I figured I'd make a pilot suit for ya. That way, you're not out fighting Titans in a T-shirt and sweatpants." Andy laughs. "But better yet, there's a compression apparatus within the boots, so you don't quite have to worry about ruining your leg braces. I managed to have just enough support built in."

Hestius puts the items back into the case, and faces Andy. "You are in my debt once again, Andy. Thank you."

"It's no big deal, dude. If you're gonna be out saving the world, best that you look cool while doing it. Almost like a real superhero!"

"I see… But how do you know whether or not it would fit?"

"I may or may not have used your armor to get a rough idea of your dimensions."

"Clever… though as much as I appreciate this, why go as far as to make this gesture?"

"Well… I care about you, dude. In a way, you've saved my life. And you're gonna keep doing that. So if anything, I'm the one who owes you."

"I understand… Regardless, I am still grateful."

"No problem, man. Anyways, Titanious is good and ready to go when you need it. I'mma go catch up on some shows." Andy pats Hestius on the shoulder as he walks past him, heading back to the island house.

Hestius looks at his new uniform again, then up at Titanious.

"This is my destiny… One that I cannot refuse. But do I really want it?"

The demigod recalls his youth– to a moment in time where all he wanted was to live amongst the gods as a protector of Olympus. He remembers walking alongside his father at age 12 through the vast glistening structures of the heavenly city.

"Are you certain he is here, father?" The redhead looks at Hephaestus.

"Perhaps he is just a little behind. He is Zeus' general, after all."

"And a general must plan his next move carefully." echoes a dark voice from behind the father and son. Marching towards them, Ares reveals himself.

Hephaestus and the pre-teen Hestius turn and face the god of war.

"It is good to see you, brother." the fire god exclaims.

"Likewise, and Hestius, too." the vampiric warrior fixates on the demigod. "How have you been, little one?"

"As you can see, he is little, no more!" Hephaestus laughs.

"I have been well, sir." Hestius responds.

"Come. Walk with me, you two." Ares commands.

The three wander across the city, and find themselves faced with a view of the countryside from the mountainous regions.

"Ares." Hephaestus calls. "Hestius… he–"

"Wants to become a warrior." He interrupts.

"… Yes. I understand he is young, but–"

"One cannot be too young to possess agency over his own fate. If your boy wishes to serve the gods in pursuit of righteousness, then it is only natural that he walks this path. Besides, the scouts I recruit are normally brash, spoiled, and lack the heart to truly stand for themselves. No different from a human– the only difference is that the blood of gods that course in their veins supposedly grants them a sense of entitlement." Ares turns to face them, and looks at Hestius. "But your boy… if what you say is true, I have no doubt that he would make for a fine warrior."

"You have practically seen him grow. Are you certain of this?"

"Allow me to ask him, myself." Ares treads toward the young Hestius, kneeling before him. "Hestius… as my nephew, I must warn you that the path you seek is one of great adversity. It is specifically designed to break you, before putting you back together, and crushing you once more. While this path can kill a man, it crumbles the fortitude of us gods. You will learn to survive by yourself, and yourself only. You may make new brothers, but also many enemies. Hestius, son of Hephaestus and Aphrodite, whose namesake is the fiery spirit of Hestia, is this the path you *truly* seek?"

Hestius recomposes himself for his response. "I swear by Zeus, my mother, my father, and all of Olympus. Even if I were to be struck down, I will do whatever it takes to defend this world from whatever evil may come!"

The war god gives a slight smirk before standing back up, facing his brother. "You raised him well. Bring him to my arena at dawn."

Hephaestus and Ares nod at one another, the latter parting ways with him and his son as they watch on.

Three more weeks go by on the island. Weeks of combat training and conditioning. Weeks of testing Titanious' physical capabilities, such as speed, power, and strength. Weeks of Andy tinkering around with ways to improve the machine's mobility to compensate for its massive bulk. Weeks of Hestius getting smacked around by

Hades' staff at the smallest of errors, with the addition of lectures. Weeks of Andy showing off different comics and superheroes to Hestius. Weeks of Andy trying to perfect dishes he has never learned how to make with Hades breathing down his neck. Weeks of peace. Weeks of growth. The Titans have yet to trigger another attack.

The next morning comes. Hestius exits from his bed to perform a series of stretches on a mat beside it. Going from pretzel stretches to quad stretches, hamstring stretches, external hip rotations, seal stretches, as well as cat, butterfly, and frog stretches, pigeon holds, and knee hugs. Andy is still sound asleep, but on the couch as opposed to his bed, due to passing out in the middle of watching *Primal Warrior Draco Azul: The Animation*. After performing his mobility routine, Hestius changes into his training outfit, fixes himself a quick glass of water, and makes his way to meet with Hades on the beach. Upon his arrival, the redheaded pilot meets with the god of the dead, who has a boulder at his side, watching the sunrise.

Hades turns to Hestius. "You have come a ways since you awakened. But as you know, our training is still far from over. While you have gained some of your old strength back, your endurance, especially in your legs, still needs more work. We will continue your combat training, and push your physicality. But now, it is time we push a little harder."

Hestius nods. "Understood. What do you have for me today?"

"You are to push this boulder." Hades gestures to the large stone at his side.

Hestius furls his brow. "Only push the boulder?"

"Indeed. Push it until it has traveled a single kilometer. That will be all." Hades proceeds to walk off.

"Wait!" Hestius tries to verbally stop him. "You are not going to stay?"

Hades glances back at the redhead. "I will know whether or not you have finished."

The god of the dead marches on, and Hestius looks back at the large stone before him, slowly walking to it.

"Just the boulder? Surely there must be something else to it, right?"

Hestius lowers his center of gravity, placing his hands on the boulder's face, and using the power from his chest, shoulders, triceps, core, and feet, the giant rock budges. But not by a lot. In fact, Hestius barely managed to move it even half a foot.

"Ah... I see..." Hestius steps back to examine the stone. *"This may take a while."*

Hestius drives the boulder along through the white sands at a steady pace. Not too aggressive to wear himself out, but not too light in his efforts, either. The heat of the sun pours onto the land mass, and as a result, shines onto the redhead. With every push, a heavy breath, and drops of sweat. Before he knew it, Hestius had finally reached a quarter of his one kilometer goal, and decided to stop and catch his breath. He feels his lips, and notices that each of his breaths are a bit shorter than usual.

"I did not drink enough water this morning... I suppose I could just go back and get some– No... if I stop, then Hades would think that I quit today... Though, he would probably understand if I explain, yes? Ugh, then he may just lecture me again, telling me that I am undisciplined. That damn old man. Or, I could simply idle until enough time has passed. Actually, I would have fully recovered by then. It would be noticeable. I could probably fake it... but why lie in the first place? That goes against my principles."

Hestius slowly fixates at the boulder again.

"This is a test. Hades is testing me– my strength, and also my will... It looks as if there is only one way out. I will have to keep going."

The redhead begins to push again.

After some time, another quarter has been reached, leaving Hestius at the halfway point. The young man drops to his knees on the hot sand as the sun climbs through the sky. He starts taking slow, deep breaths, all while his muscles ache due to the lack of hydration.

"Halfway… All I need to do is bring it back, and I am finished."

Hestius slowly climbs back to his feet and moves on around to the opposite side of the boulder, and gets into position. After taking several more inhales and exhales, he pushes again.

As he and the stone continue to travel, the sweat from his body drenches his clothes into a wet, sopping mess. Meanwhile, the rock resonates with the rays of the sun, resulting in a reaction that causes it to slowly reach higher in temperature. While this heat radiating from the stone would leave a mortal in pain, being the son of Hephaestus is serving Hestius well, for it has no effect on him.

Instead of stopping for a break at three quarters of the way through his goal, the redhead decides to persist. He chooses to keep going, taking slow, large, and powerful steps as he heaves forward. However, Hestius' dehydration would get the best of him. Upon pushing on his left foot, at approximately a fifth away from finishing, Hestius feels a shock in his left calf– a shock that begins to tighten around the back section of his lower leg, but with a sharp piercing-like sensation. This feeling is enough to leave Hestius in shock himself, as he cries out in pain before collapsing onto the fiery hot sand below him. He is pinned onto the ground, clueless as to what to do. He tries resisting the pain, but it only becomes stronger. It feels as if his leg is about to explode.

"Agh, damn! What is this!? What is happening to me!? Why does my leg hurt so much!?"

Hestius breathes rapidly, trying his best to get rid of the pain, but after enduring so much fatigue and exhaustion, all he can do is lie on the scorching ground. The redhead slowly but surely gives into the pain, letting his body do everything it can to relax, hoping the ache would fade away… and then it does. Hestius' leg finally feels free from the pain. He slowly gets back up, and gets back to work, but with more caution, in case something like that were to occur once more. Hestius pushes one last time, and meets his one kilometer goal for the day.

Upon returning to the beach house, a sweat-soaked and somewhat limping Hestius is greeted by Hades, who looks down at him.

"Excellent, young warrior. However, it appears you have finished longer than I had hoped."

Hestius, through his breaths, replies in confusion. "Longer than you hoped?"

"I suspect that you had not been taking good enough care for your being? Especially when it comes to consuming a meal prior to training, and water?"

"How do you–?"

"It is very evident. You know better, boy. You must not grow lazy in correspondence to your development. It is a paradox that shall lead you to nowhere but a path of a fool who is responsible for his own hindrance."

Hestius sighs. "Yes, Hades."

"Now, go eat. Next time, you shall do two kilometers."

The redhead wipes his face, almost to hide his distasteful reaction.

"Are you giving me attitude, boy?" Hades brings his face closer to his.

Hestius is taken aback. "N-No, Hades, I-I am just tired, sweaty, fatigued, and exhausted!"

"That is what I thought." The old master retracts.

Hestius passes Hades, and enters the house.

"It really will not get easier... Yet, I do not have much of a choice. This is how I become stronger. No time for comfort."

CHAPTER V: CHANGE

Upon returning to the island home, Hestius gathers several bags of ice, and brings them to the bathroom. He turns on the water to let it run, and fill the tub. After some time had passed, Hestius twists the handle to off, and grips his fingers onto one of the thick, plastic bags before tearing it open, letting ice cubes spill into the water. The redhead repeats this process for the remaining bags. Once finished, he tosses the empty bags into the trash, strips bare, and slowly steps into the tub, pushing air out from his body in response to the cool temperature as he descends his body into the freezing water, and to a seated position, cautiously leaning back against the end behind him. Several breaths and tense muscles later, Hestius begins to relax, putting himself at ease, and succumbing to the ice within the water. Gently, he shuts his eyes.

Slowly, he envisions himself surrounded by the vastness of the ocean, gradually sinking deeper into the darkness below, as the sea cools his body. However, the depths feel bottomless, leading to a void of nothingness. But, there is an air of peacefulness. Everything is quiet, and still. Nothing but the echoes of the slow heartbeat of Hestius. The blood that courses through his veins. Then, his mind begins to race. Deep within, strange sounds are heard.

They almost sound like monsters. In fact, they are monsters… the ones he had slain. The beastly cries of despair from Oceanus and Tethys imprint themselves into the redhead's psyche. Suddenly, Hestius finds himself face-to-face with a giant skull… the skull of Oceanus and his razor-sharp teeth. Floating behind him, the bloodied, bruised, and burnt corpse of Tethys. The two figures draw closer to him. The skull unhinges his maw, guiding it towards Hestius' body, as the body of Tethys starts to curl around them.

Hestius releases his eyes, and realizing he had submerged himself in the icy water, the redhead immediately pulls himself out with a heavy gasp, and starts panting, grabbing onto the sides of the tub. His heartbeat is rapid, but eventually calms himself to be in sync with his breathing. The young man looks at his reflection in the water, but is reminded of the sight of Tethys' body lying dead on the stone structure at the bottom of the ocean. He tightens his eyelids for a moment, lowering his head, as if to get rid of the memory that lingers.

Later, Hestius sits at the kitchen table after helping himself with an apple as the TV runs, showing a news story of sudden tremors in Mount Ossa. Caressing the red fruit takes Hestius back to the time he first arrived in Athens, when a kind vendor had helped him with a peach. However, upon chomping down on the apple, his mind goes to the point in his battle with Oceanus, when he attempted to devour that same man. He chews on the piece he had removed with his teeth, and finally swallows.

"My life, or theirs… Even when many are at stake…"

Down the stairs swings Andy, greeting Hestius, who looks down upon his apple.

"Yo, Hes!"

Hestius snaps out of focus, and looks to Andy. "Hello, Andy."

"You've been watching the TV, right?" Andy gestures back to the screen with his thumb.

"I have been listening, but not carefully. Why?"

"Well, as you see, there's tremors going on in Calypso Canyon. Doesn't seem out of the ordinary, right?"

"I suppose."

"After all, the probability of an earthquake in that area isn't impossible. In actuality, it isn't likely, but it's not like it can't ever happen."

"I see… What are you suggesting?"

"It's been a while since any of the Titans attacked, right? What, like a month or so?"

"About that much, yes."

Andy gives Hestius a look, as if to say 'connect the dots.'

Hestius looks to the side, furling his brow, and looks at Andy again. "We must find Hades."

"I heard." The elderly god enters the room. "It is very likely that it is another attack, but in the guise of a natural occurrence. I must say, it is a smart tactic."

"I guess after trying to come from the sea, they're going through land this time around." Andy holds his chin. "Makes sense… if Oceanus was sent for recon, and failed, they'd use a creature who'd be more fitting for the job… but why didn't they just send that one in the first place… You'd think that'd be easier, right?"

"It is an interesting strategy." Hades turns to Hestius. "Maybe by learning your capabilities, they would traverse where we least expect."

"That still does not seem right…" Hestius suggests. "It is possible, but I am not certain… I still feel there is more to this."

"Only one way to find out, boy." says Hades. "Though, I suspect that tremors must be the work of the Titan Iapetus."

"Iapetus!?" Hestius calls out. "Are you certain of this!?"

"When Ares forced me to exile, he was among the Titans who had joined the alliance."

The three of them proceed to look at the TV monitor, showing a broadcast from the mountain.

"I am here at the site on helicopter, and while the tremors haven't necessarily been catastrophic for the most part, they have been random, but there was only one instance that would have been very dangerous if any wildlife or hikers were nearby. Thankfully, nobody is hurt, though the tremors don't seem like they're gonna stop anytime now, but we'll be back for more updates. Back to you, Channel 72! ... Wait, what's th–?"

The broadcast makes a cut.

"Mount Ossa is currently evacuated and off-limits as we speak, and we will continue to cover more. While it is unknown, plenty have speculated that these tremors may be connected to the sudden creature attacks from last month, but there is no confirmation as of this moment. Some even believe the mysterious red robot from both attacks may appear once again, but there is no evidence at this time, and all we can do is wait."

"Guess it's time to suit up, guy." Andy nudges Hestius.

Hestius gives Andy a nod before exiting the room.

"And don't forget your pilot suit!" Andy shouts.

About one hour later, Titanious emerges from upon reaching Calypso bay and proceeds to scale up a cliff before it. The giant machine grips and pulls itself up the tall, earthy structure, and eventually reaches the top, greeted by a valley of steep plateaus. As it begins to march, Hestius scans his eyes across the green hills in search of any traces of destruction.

Hestius thinks to himself. *"I never once took Iapetus as being wrathful… Perhaps he is in this for his own means?"*

Having yet to find a trail, the mech continues to traverse through the vast, rigid openness of the valley before meeting the edge of the canyon. Before Titanious, a beautiful subsection of the earth, full of forestry and small bodies of water that brought it to life. However, Hestius notices cracks in the canyon floor. The crimson goliath reaches down at the cliff before it, and leaps forward, scaling down to the canyon depths, and sticks a landing. The red giant walks, following the tremors to see where they lead. The canyon itself stretches on for what seems to be an eternity, almost like a maze of varying cliffs that surround the premises.

Suddenly, while following the trail of wreckage left behind, Hestius starts to feel a rumble. A slight one. A quiet one. However, the rumble becomes more rapid. Something is coming, and it is directly beneath him. Upon realizing this, Titanious jumps out of the way, and out from the Earth below, explodes a colossal, horned, almost dinosaurian quadruped, covered in green moss and charcoal gray stone on his brown, leather-like body that allows him to blend in with his surroundings, with spikes running down its arms and legs that help it to travel underground. The creature is about 60 meters long from head to rear, and 40 meters tall, thanks to his gigantic hunch. The Titan Iapetus reveals himself to the vermilion knight, and upon landing on his four legs, puts on an intimidation display, ready to fight his opponent.

Titanious pushes itself up, and assumes a wrestler's position, and slowly orbits around Iapetus to keep its distance from the feral beast, immediately choosing defense in this bout. The large Titan lets out a monstrous roar before sprinting at the mech, and leaps to attack. Thankfully, Hestius is quick enough to duck down, causing the monster to miss. However, upon landing on the side of a cliff behind Titanious, Iapetus pounces back onto the colossal machine, knocking it into the ground with his weight, and begins to slash away at its back. Trying to recover from the sudden whiplash, Hestius pulls the switches in front of him, and uses Titanious' arms to grab onto the beast on his back by the front left leg, and pulls itself up onto its right leg before hurling him over its shoulder, and onto his back. Before he could reorient itself back onto his feet, Titanious jumps on top of the Titan, trying to configure itself and Iapetus into a position resembling a half nelson, wrapping its right arm around the monster's head, and the left around his body, driving its center of mass onto the creature in hopes to pin him to the ground. Iapetus retracts his hind legs and drives them into the ruby warrior's abdomen, launching him away, immediately burrowing into the ground. Titanious lands on its back, and pushes itself up with its hands, only to feel the Earth tremble beneath it, as the creature's torso emerges, and forcefully pulls it into the trench below. The mech quickly pulls and kicks away, leaving only its torso above the surface. As the machine starts to pull himself out of the hole created by Iapetus, the Titan pops out from Titanious' side, and zooms across its face, delivering a slash from its arm spikes. Despite this, Titanious persists, as its full body is now back on land. Iapetus charges for another attack as the mech gets back up. The creature jumps at the crimson goliath.

"I have you, now!" cries Hestius.

Titanious shifts downward to catch the beast, just like it did with Oceanus. However, seeing through this, Iapetus curls itself into a large sphere, and crashes into the mech, causing it to collapse beneath him, as the monster proceeds to roll around the canyon and strike Titanious as it struggles to post itself. Blow after blow, Iapetus plows through the red giant from every possible angle. Eventually, Iapetus uncurls itself back, and puts on another intimidation display, as Titanious slowly gets onto its feet.

"Come on, beast!" the pilot shouts.

Iapetus dashes once more, and rolls onto a ball again, speeding toward the mech, who staggers its feet, draws its elbows down to its lats, and fires its palms into the Titan upon impact, and starts bull-rushing it backward. As it drives, Iapetus swiftly pulls away to catch Titanious off balance. Thankfully, the ruby warrior stops itself from being unstable, and maintains a stance to prepare for Iapetus' next move. The creature reveals itself again, and stalks around the vermilion knight. Hestius watches, moving Titanious in coordination with Iapetus. The two giants pace slowly, eyeing one another, stepping in circles. This is when something clicks in Hestius.

"Is he... idling? Is he waiting on me to make a move?"

Iapetus growls, sidestepping.

"I do not understand... Why wait for me to attack...? No. It must be a trap. I am in his domain. For being the son of Gaia, he sure is resourceful."

Several minutes pass. The two eventually come to a stop. The creature lets out a snarl before it decides to turn around and burrow underground again. Hestius is in a state of both shock and confusion.

"Did he just... flee? Why retreat? He had the upper hand!"

Titanious relaxes itself, and stands more upright, and waits another minute.

"I guess it is over..."

Suddenly, the ground beneath the mech begins to shake.

"What!?"

The Earth splits open below Titanious. Failing to grab a ledge, the entire area of the canyon floor collapses underground, creating a deep, wide trench. Now, the canyon has become much deeper than before, by about half a kilometer. At the bottom lies the crimson goliath, surrounded by debris.

"Dammit… so it was a trap."

Titanious slowly gets up, and Hestius looks around, searching for Iapetus, only to see a series of tunnels in the canyon walls. The crimson goliath assumes a fighter's stance, slowly pacing around, watching each tunnel. Suddenly, Hestius hears rumbles from the creature's caverns. Titanious swifts around to face each entry that emits a sound.

"He wants me to follow him, only drawing me more towards a disadvantage. I cannot give up my defense. He clearly knows what he is doing, so it is only a matter of time before he decides to attack again if I wait around."

The red giant turns to each tunnel as Iapetus digs through each one.

"Wait… this is just like when I fought Tethys… This cannot be a coincidence– this is just like before! Iapetus must be planning something, and it appears he is not coming out anytime soon."

Titanious continues to step around.

"I have no choice… I must go after him."

Titanious proceeds to enter one of the tunnels dug by Iapetus, traveling into the Earth. Unfortunately, the path is pure black– nothing is visible in sight, but the exit behind. The vermilion knight activates its illumination system, and continues to march, hoping to lure Iapetus. Suddenly, the ceiling trembles, and what was once the exit is then closed off by fallen earth.

"So you do want me to come after you."

Titanious punches upward at the ground above it, and starts to climb its way through to another passageway. Upon reaching the tunnel above, the exit also gets shut by debris. With Hestius growing agitated, he decides to have Titanious make a passage through the wall beside him, and toward another tunnel. This also gets closed off. Instead of making another move, Hestius thinks to himself.

"Everytime I move to another tunnel, he awaits. Now he must be after me!"

Climbing through the tunnel comes Iapetus, pulling himself through, closing in on Titanious who tries to catch him, but the beast charges on. The two giants then burst through the closing of the tunnel, and out into the earthy arena laid out by the monster. After landing on its back with the Titan on top of it, the ruby warrior quickly grabs the beast by the neck.

"Found you!"

Hestius starts getting flashbacks to the end of his bout with Tethys and her bloodied body, as the memory had sprung out of the echoes in his mind. Hestius' heart sinks, and begins to shiver.

"No... that feeling again... Why now!?"

Titanious' grip weakens, and Iapetus scurries away by digging into the ground. Then, the voice of Hades fills his brain. Words of wisdom that encourage him to fight, but remind Hestius of the harsh reality of the ongoing battle he has found himself within. The Titan comes out once again, launching itself from the canyon wall, and onto the mech's back, as he then grabs onto its shoulders, hurls itself forward, and upon landing on his feet, Iapetus chucks Titanious into the wall.

"I promised I would not falter... Why am I lacking the strength I need?"

The beast gallops on over and grabs the red giant by the head, while also pinning its torso into the wall, and starts to slam its head repeatedly into the earth.

"Please, ... father, ... mother, ... give me strength...!"

Hestius is then taken back in time– over 25 centuries ago. He was just 8 years old when the mighty Hercules had slain the Hydra. Up to this point, Hestius' teacher from his youth, Gabriella, had taught the young demigod the beauties of life on Earth. And seeing a large, serpentine dragon with multiple heads become slain at the hands of a powerful warrior– especially one such as Hercules– had stunned the boy.

"It is a true shame, indeed." Gabriella says sadly.

The young Hestius looks up at the deep violet-haired motherly figure, who looks down at him as if she knew how he had felt. She caresses his cheek with her gentle palm.

"These creatures never ask for this. Nor do they want a part in our affairs… But unfortunately, little one, that is their tragedy. It is up to us to take care of one another– even if it means ridding the world of such lovely creatures, regardless if they mean any harm or not. And the reality is that these beasts… these animals… They are just too big to live in our world. Too big to share a home with. There is a balance that we must keep– a balance that ensures a future for us and the things we love. These creatures, full of life, live on their accord, but serve us, and help us understand who we are. And one day, Hestius, you will be faced with hard choices to make. But these choices will help you grow. Not only will they benefit you, but they will benefit others as well."

Hestius looks down, almost teary-eyed. Gabriella kneels down, and wipes his face with her hand, holding his shoulders.

"It is important that not only we, but you keep living… Can you promise me that, little one?" she smiles.

Little Hestius nods his head. Gabriella pulls him into her embrace, as he slowly wraps his arms around her back, and sniffles into her bosom.

"True strength and compassion lies in the fortitude of those who are capable of facing the most difficult challenges. One day, you will have that strength."

"My life, or theirs… Them, or humanity… I… must… not… die!!!"

Hestius begins to cry out. Suddenly, an orange glow begins to trace around Titanious' inner workings, as its body begins to climb to high temperatures, causing its metallic chassis to become scorching hot. Iapetus quickly reacts and immediately backs off and away from the mech. The crimson goliath pushes itself out from the canyon wall, and turns to face the Titan, now with an ocher, fiery glow surrounding its body, and eyes shining white. Titanious has finally reached Fotia Alpha— a state where the mech is embedded in a blaze that is the result of Hestius' ever-growing will and spiritual strength.

"This is my world." the teary-eyed Hestius cries. "And it does not belong to you, anymore!"

Iapetus lets out a roar and slowly backs up, facing the mech. Titanious proceeds to step forward, and walk in the Titan's direction. The burning aura of the red giant grows brighter, almost blinding the beast. Iapetus decides that he has no choice, but to attack– the monster starts sprinting at the robot. Titanious, with Hestius letting out a battle cry, charges at the beast. Right before they collide, Iapetus launches itself at the vermilion knight, who then lowers his leverage for a tackle. Upon impact, Titanious wraps its arms around the beast, and drives it into the ground on his back. The monster screeches from the searing metal skin of the scarlet soldier. The burning sensation emitting from the machine is enough to pin Iapetus to the ground as it desperately squirms around to try and get away, all while the mech has the creature trapped between its knees as they squeeze and sizzle against the Titan.

"I will not ask for forgiveness. At the very least, I just hope you understand why it has come to this."

Titanious raises its right hand in the air. Shortly, the clenched fist of the blazing warrior begins to spark and burst into flames.

"I do not want to kill you…" Hestius breaks further into tears. "But I cannot let you live. Not in a place like this!" The red giant then proceeds to slam its fist down at the creature, and right when the attack lands, a massive explosion erupts, covering the trench in smoke and fire. This is the power of the Titan Buster.

Moments later, as the dust and smoke begin to settle, Titanious has returned to its original state– its orange glow being absent. As for the Titan Iapetus– reduced to ashes. Its resting place will forever be within the canyons of Mount Ossa. Hestius pants heavily, exhausted, as he recollects his emotions after the battle.

"Thank you, Titanious." he says. "Thank you, father… and thank you, mother."

Both the demigod and his colossal machine look up towards the clouds above.

"Farewell, Iapetus… Your soul may not forgive me, but I hope you understand why it has come to this."

Slowly, the mech rises to its feet, and proceeds to make its way outside of the massive crater, and eventually Mount Ossa.

Later that night, back on Keros Island, Andy is touching up on Titanious for repairs.

"So let me get this straight," he says. "Titanious just started glowing? Like it powered up!?"

"Indeed." Hestius replies, crossing his arms. "I suppose it read and adapted to my emotions."

"Titanious is an extension of your power." enters Hades. "While it is built for fighting, it is a tool that allows you to amplify your spirit. Remember, it is powered by your will and courage."

"That must have been why it had grown weak when–" Hestius stops himself.

"When what?" asks Hades, looking down at the redhead.

Hestius takes a small breath. "When my mind was not on the battle."

"Boy, whether you have the strength of ten-thousand men or ten-thousand gods, your greatest war will forever be the one in your mind. And in every waking moment of your life, you must conquer it."

"Understood." Hestius bows his head subtly.

"The very form you had tapped into with Titanious is called Fotia Alpha." Hades adds.

"Fotia Alpha?"

"Indeed. Your father created it to achieve three stages of power– Alpha is the first, followed by Fotia Delta.

And when the heavens shine down upon you, Titanious shall ascend to Fotia Omega, where it is at its strongest."

"Really? I am surprised my father never informed me of this power...."

"Because you are still growing, young one. While your body may have matured, your mind and spirit have yet to reach their potential. Soon enough, you will push Titanious to its limits."

Andy enters the cockpit of Titanious, and scans his eyes around before locking his vision onto the seat, levers, and switches at the center. The young engineer gently holds his chin, allowing his thoughts to race back and forth. Eventually, he snaps his fingers, and peeks out of the mech.

"Yo, Hes!" Andy calls out.

Hestius looks up at him, and replies. "What is it?"

"Just wanna let you know that repairs are gonna take a *bit* longer than expected."

"What do you mean? Is something wrong?"

"Not really, but I have an idea. Though, I will have to take the control center back to my garage in Athens if you don't mind."

"Very well... I trust that you will ensure that Titanious will be ready to go."

"Of course!"

"Do you need the Scylla to take you back?" pitches Hades.

"Uh…" Andy responds. "I'll find a boat."

CHAPTER VI: GIFT

In the depths of the underworld, where the charred landscape reaches far and wide, lies an arena. And in the amphitheater, the throne of its ruler, clad in black armor, as souls enter. Ares, the god of war, rests in his seat with an arm propped, his face against his hand, eyeing the essence of Oceanus, Tethys, and Iapetus, as they loom in the clouds of this hellscape.

"Sire!" shouts a large armored demonic humanoid, donning bat-like features. Kronos, the king of the Titans, Kronos, enters the arena before bowing to his commander.

Ares' eyes drag to the Titan king's direction.

"Our reconnaissance operation has failed once more. What are your orders for now?"

The war god releases a sigh, and raises his head. "No. We have what we need to move forward."

"No, my lord?" perks Kronos.

"Oceanus may have been sent to observe the terrain, as were his wife and Iapetus… But I would be foolish to release them alone."

"How do you mean?"

"I suspected the half-breed would be alive after all these years, and his wretched machine, too. Yet, it is fascinating."

"I see…" Kronos lowers his head again. "But, what is it about the half-breed that intrigues you?"

"His mighty potential… I only wish for it to not stand in our way. So I sent Themis to observe and gather information on these confrontations."

"Themis?" Kronos questions urgently. "Where is she? Shall I summon her?"

"No need. She is in the field as we speak."

Kronos pauses for a brief moment. "Sire, I understand the terms that were in place when we formed our alliance, but why was I not informed of Themis' activity?"

"Do you not trust your master?" Ares stares down Kronos.

Kronos swallows his breath. "Forgive me, my lord. I did not mean to question your methods."

"Stand down for now, Kronos." Ares clasps his hands together, interlocking his fingers as he leans back against his throne. "You have done plenty more than enough."

Kronos rises to his feet. "Only to serve you, my lord. May the world become yours." The Titan king gives a salute, and proceeds to make his exit.

The god of war looks in Kronos' direction as he draws away from the arena.

"Not just mine." he utters to himself with a slight smirk.

Hestius faces the ocean waves as he watches the moon and stars above. He locks his eyes to the constellations, as if to see through the heavens. It is almost as if he is searching for the spirits of those who had fallen during the war on Olympus, and those he has fought. An act to ensure that these souls are at peace. Hestius takes a breath, as his vision hovers toward a mostly repaired Titanious.

Father, I know you gave me Titanious so I could fight on my own. But I have come to realize that even having such power, the adversity I face only grows more difficult. Perhaps, this is what you have prepared me for. So that one day, when your guidance becomes absent, I am to forge my own path. And father, I want you to know that even though you are not here, you are helping me. Everyday, despite my injuries, I am stronger than before. And as I become stronger, so does Titanious. In my last battle, I've experienced a sort of... emotion. I cannot quite describe it, but for the first time since I had awoken in this new world, my mind was clear. I felt sorrow, but I knew very well what I needed to do. I was focused, but I was willing to push through the pain. My heart was on fire, and Titanious erupted in response. Perhaps it is not just a measure of my strength, but my will. At that moment, I did not falter. I suppose what I am trying to say is thank you. You have provided enough tools for me, and I will continue to use them, and I will be certain that you continue to rest as peacefully as possible to the best of my ability.

Hestius looks to the moon for a moment, and makes his way to the island home, where he then traverses to him and Andy's room.

Andy, who is sitting at his desk illuminated by a lamp, takes notice of his roommate's entrance. "'Sup, Hes?"

"Evening." Hestius fixates onto his nerdy companion, only to draw his attention to a small device on Andy's desk with curiosity. "What is that?"

"Oh, this?" Andy raises the device– a modified cell phone that he has tinkered with all day. "Just a little surprise. Well, if it works that is." He laughs nervously.

"I see… by any chance, do you know when Titanious will be ready?"

"Ah! About that… I took apart the control center, and moved all the parts to my garage."

"You mean it's not here?"

"I'm about to get to that." Andy reaches down to a drawer, and pulls out a silver wrist device with black tracings, and shows it off to Hestius. "I want you to put this on for me real quick."

Hestius looks at the strange device, before agreeing to Andy's request, clasping it onto his arm, as it is a snug fit.

"Perfect!" Andy jumps a little. "Now, and I know it's a big favor, but you mind running an errand for me?"

"What is it?"

"I'm gonna send you on a little mission. See, it's back at my garage in Athens, and I just need you to calibrate that little wrist device to it. Shouldn't take too long."

"You want me to go alone at night?"

"I wouldn't quite say alone. That's where this is gonna come in." Andy raises the modified cell phone with a smirk. "Figured we could use a little comm system, so that we're not just hoping you don't die out there."

Hestius crosses his arms and shuts his eyes to process this proposal. "Very well. I'll go."

"Sweet!" Cries Andy. "And FYI, I suggest you don't take the Scylla to get there. That device is still a prototype, so it's not exactly waterproof just yet. I'd go by boat instead."

Hestius travels to one of the island's ports for a way to Athens. He proceeds to set foot in one of the boats, and begins to set sail. As the vessel pierces through the gentle waves, the redhead decides to lie down on the deck, and gazes upon the stars once more. Just the same as before, as if to send a message to those in the afterlife. After staring up at the night sky for a few minutes, he then takes a deep breath.

Mother... I am unsure what to say... I want to thank you, but... I just wish I had not been so cruel when I found out the truth. I realized what was at hand, but it was already too late. I know very well you would do anything for me the same as father. I just wish I could apologize while you were still here. The tools you have provided me are just as vital as father's. I do not know how you have passed, but I want you to know that I truly am sorry for my rashness, and that all those years of teaching have been of use. I just had not become aware of it until now. I hope that when you left this Earth, the passage to the Elysian Plain was a calm one. Thank you.

Hestius clenches his fist, remaining stillness is held for some time, until the traveler takes another breath and releases the tension contained in his body. Time passes as he is left alone with his thoughts, up until the young warrior reaches his destination. Upon stepping into the city of Athens, Hestius pulls a small map of his whereabouts from his right pocket, eyeing the trace Andy left for him to get to his garage. However, this is only proven somewhat useful as the wreckage from Oceanus' attack has still yet to be reconstructed, and is still "under quarantine" according to some of the signage laid across the vicinity. Despite this, Hestius insists on searching for his ally's garage. Minutes go by as he travels through the dark alleys in the night, navigating through debris from his battle months prior.

Suddenly, Hestius feels a wave of paranoia looming above him— something does not seem right. He stops in his tracks, and scans his surroundings, only to find nothing. The demigod then carries on with caution, carefully looking around. The feeling of someone or something else being present had not left his mind. Eventually, his ears feel a slight trigger— a faint scuffle that is not too far behind him. Hestius stops once again to register the validation of his suspicion: he is being followed. The redhead remains calm, takes another gander at his map, and decides to take an alternate route; but instead, he moves away from his destination as a means to try and catch his stalker in their tracks. However, it is not long until he finds himself on a ledge of an area that had been rendered unrecognizable from its original state. The map is of no use, as it is nothing but a field of emptiness and rubble. Seeing this before him, Hestius turns back. But, before he could continue, the demigod is greeted by the appearance of his follower. A woman donning a gray trench coat, and dark shades to hide her visage arrives. Her boots stroll through the stone cold ground with intent as she approaches Hestius.

"Who are you?" he questions.

The woman does not answer.

"Why are you following me?"

Still no answer.

"Don't come any further!" he cries out as he slowly backs away.

She continues like a lioness tracking her prey, getting closer to her target.

"You leave me no choice." Hestius staggers, and assumes a defensive position.

"Have I?" The woman immediately drives the heel of her foot into his sternum, knocking the wind out of him as he launches backward into the crater.

Hestius rolls all the way down to the wreckage floor, desperately trying to catch his breath. The woman leaps down after him.

The redhead climbs up to his knees and looks up at her. "Ares sent you after me…"

"Yes." She says, raising her right arm across her body. "And I cannot let you live." The mysterious woman flicks her arm back down as a blade emerges from the sleeve of her coat.

Hestius swiftly pushes himself back to his feet, and takes on his stance again. The woman lunges into him for a strike, only for Hestius to parry her attack, and charges his fist toward her torso for an uppercut. The woman quickly catches the incoming hand, and Hestius immediately pulls back, as she swings her blade toward him. The redhead sees this, and swiftly leans back, barely missing the woman's sword, but results in his body stumbling onto the ground. As Hestius scrambles to get back to his feet, the woman performs another swipe with her blade in a downward angle, to which the demigod shuffles away. The woman aims her sword toward Hestius, slowly approaching him before taking a quick step while circling the edge of her blade in the air, leading to an upward slash. Hestius twists to evade the attack, ducking underneath her arm before grabbing onto it with his left hand. The demigod hastily rotates around, pulling her with his hand, using his right to drive the woman over his shoulder and into the ground. Hestius releases her, and shifts backward in his stance. During this motion, the blade of the woman's sword grazes against the metal of the young warrior's braces on his legs. Hestius slowly orbits around her, watching as the woman slowly posts herself on a knee, supporting herself with her sword. Suddenly, she freezes– calmly, rather.

Hestius keeps his eyes on her, but with a hint of confusion. Slowly, he treads toward the woman, before taking a heavy step to ground himself before lunging in for a tackle. Unfortunately, the woman quickly notices this, and slashes at the brace of his planted leg, cutting through the metal, rendering that leg useless. Before he could go airborne, Hestius collapses back to the ground, and tries to hobble his way back up. The woman quickly turns around, and proceeds to charge at him, aiming to attack his legs, now having discovered his weakness. She begins to jab and swing her sword repeatedly as the demigod struggles to back away and avoid her strikes. One of these strikes lead to her blade getting wedged between his opposite leg and the brace. Realizing this, the woman twists the blade's position, so that the edge would slice his leg as she pulls back. Hestius cries out in response now that his mobility has further been restricted. Unsure what to do, the redhead starts to flee with imperfection, as the woman follows from behind.

As Hestius limps away from his opponent, a sound starts to emit from the wrist device that Andy gave him, almost as if it were an alarm. He shifts his attention to the device, as the red bulb on its side begins to blink. The demigod looks at it while trying to escape the mysterious woman, and focuses back on his objective. Once again he stumbles onto the ground, and resorts to crawling away. However, the woman is gaining up on him.

Hestius turns back to face her, and shouts. "Why are you trying to kill me!?"

The woman marches closer. "Because there is no other way."

She proceeds to raise her blade up in a manner, as if to prepare to deliver one last blow to her prey. All of a sudden, the blinking red light on Hestius' wrist device starts to beep at a higher frequency. Then higher, higher, and higher until the light turns green, and the sound is elongated for a brief moment. Immediately after, a revving sound is heard from the distance. The two fighters draw their attention to find the source. The revving then turns into the sound of a motor, coupled with the acceleration of wheels. And lastly, a strange machine appears, leaping from the ledge of the battlefield, and flies toward the mysterious woman, as it eventually collides into her, forcing her away, and onto the ground. She cries out as the machine drives over her, and maneuvers itself toward Hestius before coming to a stop. Lying before Hestius, a customized motorcycle done in the same colors as Titanious. A voice is then heard from the bike– it's Andy.

"Get on, quick!"

Without a second thought, Hestius shuffles his way over, and climbs onto the motorcycle as it starts to drive away from the fight, leaving the woman behind. The injured young warrior looks back at the woman while she tries to stand back up before they re-enter the streets.

"Sorry for the delay. I noticed you were close by, and started the calibration. What happened?"

Hestius looks at the monitors on the dashboard of the red motorcycle. "I was followed. Ares sent someone after me. They must have known about the control center."

"I see." Andy lets out a nervous laugh. "Good thing we beat them to it!"

"What do you mean? We should turn around and get to it before they do!"

"Looks like you haven't figured it out. This *is* your control center!"

"What?" Hestius is puzzled.

"I figured I'd reconstruct it using its cratonium alloy as a coat for this bike I've been working on. Now no matter what, I can see and hear everything out on the battlefield! And all thanks to that phone I've been tinkering with."

"And I'm supposed to use this for Titanious?"

"That's the fun part! And the fact that you now have a better means of getting around. Your legs look pretty busted there. Let's get you to a port and get you back here. Don't worry about steering for now– it's on autopilot."

Hestius rides the bike into the night, as it retreats back to where he had entered the city of Athens.

Lying on the sofa in the living area of the island home, Hades patches Hestius' wounds, as Andy repairs his leg braces. Occasionally, the redhead tenses up as the god of the dead runs a thread through the gash on his leg, sewing his mortal flesh back together.

"There." speaks Hades, finalizing his stitching.

Hestius limply rotates his leg to allow blood to circulate to the wound, watching it.

"Rest easy these next two days."

"Two days?" questions the demigod.

"For humans, it would be two weeks." Hades grabs a roll of tape with one hand, then Hestius' leg with the other. "Now hold still."

"But Ares could attack at any moment in that time!"

The elderly god begins to wrap a soft patch around the closed gash. "Yes, you were followed by an assassin, and I would much rather we plan our next move– but we also do not want to hinder your recovery."

"It's a good thing I caught you in time, or you *really* would've been in bad shape!" Andy performs the final touches on Hestius' leg braces. "But in the meantime, those two days will give us an excuse to work on synchronizing Crimson Magma to Titanious."

Hestius curiously looks at Andy. "Crimson Magma?"

"Oh yeah…" Andy pushes up his glasses. "That's what I called your new motorcycle. Got it from an old superhero idea I had once, but never went anywhere with it."

"Crimson Magma…" ponders Hestius. "I like the name."

"It's almost as if the raging fires of your father are with you!"

Hestius releases a small, gentle chuckle. "I suppose I will know how Helios must have felt."

"So about that lady from earlier… Looks like Ares wants you dead."

"We have stopped all of his advances up to this point." adds Hades. "It was only a matter of time before he proceeded to target you specifically."

"Let us hope he does not know of our whereabouts." Hestius replies.

"No need to worry." reassures Hades. "I made sure of that long ago." He finishes wrapping the young warrior's leg.

Hestius sets his leg down, and looks at the two. "Thank you both for your help. Once again, I am reminded that I will forever be in your debt."

"Until you take back Tartarus for me, that is, boy." Hades remarks lightly.

"It's no big deal." Andy scratches the back of his neck. "I'm just glad I can work on some projects I've been meaning to get to."

"Right." nods Hestius. "I will be sure to wake at dawn to practice… what did you call it?"

"Synchronization."

"Synchronization… I eagerly await trying your adjustments!"

"Though first, we should work on driving it without autopilot. That way, if I'm ever absent, you can control Crimson Magma. You can even call it to come to your position with your wrist device."

"It sounds like Crimson Magma is going to be very useful from here on out."

"And that's the thing about riding bikes– once you learn, you never forget!"

CHAPTER VII: ULTIMATUM

All is quiet on the shores of Keros Island. All but the soothing sounds of the sea as the waves wash over the sand, echoing through the sunlit coast. But far off within the island, a synthetic hum speeds through the rocky terrain– the rubber wheels of the beaming red motorcycle known as Crimson Magma climbs across the plains with high velocity, which only increases the more it treads on.

"Alright, looks like we've gotten the hang of steering." The small voice of Andy emits from the cycle's dashboard. "Now let's do some change in direction. When I give the signal, turn right back around."

"Understood." replies Hestius, donning his pilot suit as he rides Crimson Magma.

"Remember, you wanna lean into your turn. That way you keep control, *and* your center of mass."

"Right. Awaiting your signal."

The demigod presses on for another half mile, being sure to avoid hazards on his path.

"Now!" shouts Andy.

Hestius grips the bike's handles tightly before pulling his left elbow backwards as a means to throw himself into his desired direction, all while he keeps his body low, using the momentum of Crimson Magma to create an axis on one of its wheels to make for a nearly 180 degree rotation. Although Hestius used a bit too much force in this turn, making for a rather sloppy landing. Nevertheless, he continued to charge into the opposite direction with the motorcycle.

"Not too shabby if I say so myself. Especially for a beginner!"

"It is a little different from riding a horse, I will say!"

Crimson Magma charges forth through the mountainous regions of Keros Island.

"Setting up a path in your navigation system, Hes." alerts Andy. "Should be coming up… now."

A jagged, highlighted trail pops up on the motorcycle's GPS screen. Hestius revs up the bike some more before increasing speed, following the desired path. The demigod finds himself entering a ravine riddled with sharp turns. He proceeds to shift his body and the machine side to side, teetering back and forth at different accelerations with slight caution. Along the way, the left side of the vehicle gets chipped by the uneven mountain wall with minimal effect. Hestius tenses for a moment.

"Careful now! We're doing this so we don't have to rely on the autopilot so much!" shouts Andy from the bike's small speaker.

Hestius gives a nod, piercing more of his focus into the path as he exits the ravine with grace. From then on, it is a straight path down the plain– and in the distance, the towering titan of cratonium Titanious stands tall, facing the blue sea with an open cavity in its lower back.

"Alright, I'm recalibrating Crimson Magma to Titanious. If we pull this off, we're golden. Just do not stop!"

The rider pushes on, remaining at the same speed down the slope. Crimson Magma's system warns him of the resync; SYNCHRONIZING: 14%... 23%... 47%... 61%... 82%.... Hestius forms a sense of tunnel vision– in this place, there is only him, Crimson Magma, and Titanious. The demigod stares down the red giant as he accumulates more speed, as the rest of the world fades into darkness.

95%... 96%... 97%....

Hestius closes his eyes, and inhales inside his helmet.

"Guide me, father… Guide me, mother… Not just in the path I am on, but the path that is to come… And the one after."

Suddenly, Hestius begins to think back to his training from before the war, sword fighting with Ares himself when he was 15. The two have engaged in a furious, bladed altercation, but it is clear that the war god is going easy on the boy, whereas the demigod, under the guise of a pure-blooded immortal, is performing rather desperately. Ares is very well-aware of Hestius' imperfect form, yet continues to block off every single one of his strikes.

"We have been going for some time, boy– yet, you have not struck me." taunts Ares.

Hestius responds by gritting his teeth, and proceeds to swing his blade towards him repeatedly with more fury. But, same as before, they are useless against the mind of an arms expert as the god of war.

Suddenly, as one of the demigod's strikes hits the edge of his opponent's sword, Ares performs a maneuver that launches the blade away with his own. This move leaves Hestius wide open, his entire torso exposed, in which Ares' eyes light up, and proceeds to swing his blade directly at Hestius' midsection. The demigod is frozen, paralyzed by the sudden shock of such a weapon approaching body at a great speed, so much his mind can barely comprehend it. Yet, the stunned Hestius has no need to worry about death heading his way, for Ares immediately halted the attack right before impact. The demigod looks at the blade, still tremendously shaken.

"Ignorant. That is what you are." The war god calls.

"W-What!?"

"You are so focused on destroying your enemy that you have failed to maintain your stance, your defense, and ultimately, your mind."

"I-I see… C-Can we try again?"

"No." Ares removes his weapon. "We are done for today." he begins to march off towards the exit of the arena.

Hestius lets out a soft gasp. "W-Wait! Please!" he cries out. "I can do it, I swear!"

The god of war turns back to the boy. "You realize that if I had gone through with that strike, you would be dead by now? Imagine if such a thing occurred on the battlefield. That a pupil of mine would bring great shame to Olympus, all because he was not thinking straight!? You have yet to fully mature, boy. And at this rate, you will never graduate to the ranks of Zeus' army!"

The demigod sulks. But a small, yet fiery aura glows acutely around him. Ares takes notice, cocking his brow.

Facing his mentor, the boy insists. "Again. Please."

The god watches him for a moment, feeling the slight burning sensation of his passion. "Very well." He then treads back into his direction before assuming a stance. "Show me. Show me you understand."

"I will." Sword in his hand, Hestius takes on his defensive position, ready to attack.

"Remember, boy… Focus. Not on me, not yourself, but every fiber that surrounds you. Free your mind."

98%... 99%...

Releasing his breath, he opens his eyes, greeted by the flash of reentering reality.

100%.

SYNCHRONIZATION COMPLETE.

At this very second, Crimson Magma charges into Titanious' backside, and locks into the control apparatus. With the boiling blood of Hestius, the mech powers up, and the cavity is sealed behind him.

CRIMSON MAGMA CALIBRATION: SUCCESS.

TITANIOUS: ACTIVATED.

"Hell yeah, man!" Andy lets out through the cockpit's communication system.

In response to this successful moment, Hestius raises the right fist of Titanious before lowering itself into a combative stance.

"Well, looks like you've gotten the hang of this thing. Not only that, the radar is functioning as it needs to, and the camera system is working nicely." compliments Andy. "Now let's talk some shop."

After the test was proven to be a success, Hestius and Andy come together in their room. The two face one another on opposing sides of the geek's work desk, with a map of Greece lying on the face of it.

"Okay," says Andy "so far, the Titans have appeared in Athens, Piraeus, and Mount Ossa. Meanwhile, this lady you ran into found you in Athens while you were on your way to get Crimson Magma."

"Indeed." affirms Hestius. "It appears Ares has decided to put reconnaissance on hold. Almost as if they waited for me."

"Well, at least it seems they don't know we're here… But I don't get it." Andy scratches the side of his head. "How exactly did they know you were coming?"

"I can only conclude that every battle Titanious has faced has been surveyed."

"Oh… so they *do* know we're here…" Andy releases a deep, frustrated sigh. "That's great."

"I would not count on that, actually."

Andy cocks his brow. "What do you mean?"

"This woman… She wore the same facial apparatus as you, but it was black. Her vision was completely inhibited."

"Sunglasses?"

"Yes… But the sun was not present. It was nighttime."

"So she's blind."

"Correct. It was in the way she had fought me as well…" Hestius sits silently as he gathers his thoughts. "… Themis."

"The Titan Themis?"

"Exactly. Themis was quite close to the other gods, and eventually learned to take on a human form. It appears Ares used this as an advantage, so she could report back on the Titans' attacks out of sight."

"So here's what's bothering me… How does she survey these fights if she can't see?"

"While Themis' eyesight is not present, her other senses are heightened to compensate."

"Gotcha, gotcha…" Andy starts to hold his chin, looking down at the map. "Here's what I'm thinking: considering she waited for you in Athens, we can't really go back there as that would draw suspicion. I say we go to Argos; not too far, but enough so that she doesn't think we're onto her. We pull up, act like we're just hanging out, split, and we rendezvous at the castle. This way, we have a better chance of drawing her in. Once we get her, we can interrogate, find a way to beat Ares, and maybe save the world!"

Hestius sits still, his eyes on the map.

"... Hey, man, were you listening?"

"Your plan sounds efficient."

"Okay, cool! Let's go ahead and wait until sundown–"

"No need." The demigod interrupts. "We leave as soon as we are ready. She would likely try to blend in with the civilians, but I know what she looks like."

"Alrighty. Guess we'll board Titanious in an hour?"

One hour passes. The two young men make their exit from Keros Island, as Titanious marches on. As the machine swims to its destination, the sun begins to dim so slightly. The star inches its way toward the horizon, but ever so slightly. Finally, the two land in Argos after navigating the city sewers, with Titanious underneath the surface. Andy and Hestius roam about the streets of Argos on Crimson Magma, eyeing around for their target.

"So big coat and sunglasses, right?" asks Andy.

"Correct. Tied-up hair as well." replies Hestius.

"Are we talking a ponytail, a bun, pigtails? Any bangs? You're gonna have to be more specific."

"A bun, I suppose."

"You suppose?" Andy rolls his eyes. "Yeesh, we've got to get you caught up on modern fashion trends."

"We should remain quiet." Hestius suggests. "She can possibly hear us if she is nearby."

The two men stroll along until a particular store catches the attention of Andy.

"Speaking of fashion trends…"

They proceed to enter the fashion outlet after parking Crimson Magma outside. Andy decides to compile several combos of assorted windbreakers, leather jackets, and jeans for Hestius to try on. One could see it as a ploy to have him try on outfits based on his favorite *Masked Rider* protagonists. They decide to conclude their detour, and leave the store without buying anything. But as they head out, there is a woman sitting at the patio. Hestius and Andy walk their way towards the flashy motorcycle, but the former freezes upon seeing the woman, as she just so happens to not only be beside Crimson Magma, but Hestius immediately recognizes her. The coat, the sunglasses, the bun, yet combined with subtle bangs on the sides of her face. It *has* to be her.

"Stop." he utters softly to Andy.

Andy looks at him with confusion.

Hestius stares down the woman, who appears to be reading a novel. After a brief moment, the redheaded demigod starts treading toward her, as the woman lightly hums to herself.

"Themis." Hestius calls to her. However, he is ignored as the woman continues to read her book.

"What are you doing here?"

"Hm?" the woman looks up, facing Hestius.

"I said, what are you doing?" He steps closer.

The woman lightly jerks back. "U-Uh I-I'm just reading, is there a problem?"

Hestius shouts "Why are you following me, and tell me everything you know about Ares!"

This causes a disturbance among the surrounding public, as bystanders look on. Awkward tension builds between them, causing Hestius to look around, puzzled.

"You should go right now." the woman commands as she closes her book before making her leave.

Hestius retreats back to his partner with a hint of redness.

"Clearly that went well." Andy remarks.

"I… think that must have been who Themis based her image…" the demigod looks around, as if to get rid of his embarrassment.

"Welp. Guess we outta make our next move already. I'll catch you later." Andy turns in the opposite direction, and walks.

Hestius nods and heads back to Crimson Magma, revving it up before riding it down the street.

The sun descends further towards the world's vanishing point as Hestius steadily drifts his way out of the city, and towards the castle ruins to meet Andy, looking around to see if Themis happens to be nearby on his path. After finding nothing, the redhead drives up the hills in which the castle lies upon, slowly speeding towards its entrance, and traverses through the ruins.

"Andy." Hestius calls for his ally. "Are you here?"

A faint muffling is heard, and the demigod tenses lightly before rolling his way to the source. It is not long until he finds Andy bound and tied in rope.

"Andy!" he shouts.

"You should really know your enemy by now." a familiar voice echoes through the walls. A feminine figure steps out from the shadows, revealing herself to be the same woman from before. "We meet again, son of Hephaestus."

"You…" Hestius steps off of Crimson Magma, and assumes a fighting stance.

"I don't think that would be wise. Because you are going to do exactly as I say. Give me the location of Titanious." a blade swiftly springs out from Themis' right sleeve. "Or else the boy suffers."

Andy's silenced screaming grows louder as he squirms around.

"Themis." the redhead responds. "You were once the very symbol of justice itself. Have you truly wavered to such pettiness by playing such twisted games?"

"People have the right to take what they want, so long as it fulfills their goal. This goal being an idea of the greater good. Much like how Ares wants the Earth, I want Titanious. Is that not just in itself?"

"Tell me… why Titanious?"

"It is a vessel of your power is it not? Best to take out the bigger fish, and then squash out the vermin."

"So you want to destroy Titanious and me…"

"Whatever it takes. All I know is that you're a nuisance– but either way, I know exactly how to take care of you thanks to our fight from before. Face it, you have no way out of this; so you may as well hand over Titanious already."

Hestius looks at Andy, who is still shifting around, then back to Themis. "Very well." he relaxes his stance. "I will lead the way."

The demigod and Titan hop on Crimson Magma, as Hestius speeds off to where Titanious was hidden. Andy watches as he shakes and shouts more violently, showing immense disdain for being left behind.

The two travel underneath the city towards the location of the colossal red mech, passing through the tunnels of stone and concrete with cobwebs and rats at every corner, and a river of water splitting each pathway. Hestius and Themis commence forth until they reach a reservoir, the one where Titanious was stationed, hunched over in a seated position. The demigod proceeds to maneuver himself and the Titan through the platforms that run along the unit until they reach the giant machine's backside.

Themis removes herself from Hestius and Crimson Magma before aiming her blade at the redhead.

"Step off." she commands.

Hestius, looking in her direction, slowly climbs off the motorcycle, raising his hands, as if to gesture that she is in control now.

"You are going to tell me how to operate this machine."

"Drive into the control apparatus, and you will activate Titanious."

With her sword still pointed to the demigod, Themis saddles herself onto the bike, and slowly accelerates into the cockpit, where Crimson Magma docks itself into the mech. After the motorcycle shifts into Titanious' control system… Nothing. Themis presses different button configurations in an attempt to start the machine.

Frustrated, she summons Hestius. "Boy! Come here this instant!"

He climbs his way up to the cockpit, bearing witness to her predicament.

"You said to drive into the control apparatus. Why is it not working!?"

"Perhaps there is an error?"

"Quit your stalling, half-breed. You will tell me how to activate Titanious!"

Hestius walks toward where Crimson Magma is stationed, and glances over the control panel. "I see the problem."

Themis looks to the demigod with a mixture of both confusion and curiosity.

"This machine is not yours to command." Hestius sternly faces Themis as he grips his hand onto one of the handles of Crimson Magma, which slowly starts to power up Titanious. His body begins to glow a bright orange, bathing in the blazes of his birthright as the machine is activated. "You should go right now."

Themis takes in a shock, realizing that there is currently no way to pursue her goal of taking Titanious. All she has left is one last trump card– swiftly, she sprints out of the red giant, and heads up the reservoir towards the tunnels. Hestius brings himself aboard Crimson Magma, now in full control of Titanious as he uses the mech to turn and track Themis' trajectory. He starts punching through the reservoir walls to trap the Titan, but she is too agile, as she can easily sense when and where these strikes would land. Punch after punch, she manages to slip away, and into the tunnels, escaping the scarlet warrior for now.

Hestius uses Titanious' head to peek inside the tunnel, thanks to Andy's monitor installation inside the cockpit. At the precise moment he turns on the eye light beams to illuminate the passage, a giant fist charges toward the mech, and lands a hard punch to its face. Breaking through the reservoir walls with a powerful lunge from throwing this attack, a towering eyeless, black-haired. feminine humanoid with dark skin, donning purple armor, lined with gold accents. The strike knocks Titanious back into the wall behind it, leaving an indent from its mass. Themis, now in her Titan form, standing at 60 meters tall, struts over to the mech. She grabs the crown of the machine before pulling its head downward, and driving her knee into its face. The Titan then drags the red giant out from the wall, tossing it aside. Titanious recovers, pushing itself onto its feet as the two proceed to assume defensive positions.

Hestius uses the mech to lunge forward into a grapple, clenching the Titan by her shoulders before swinging her around their arena, to which Themis uses this to run her feet along the reservoir walls, and drive her weight back into it with a strong leap. Titanious restaggers itself, going for a bodyslam, but the Titan catches herself with her hands, and presses against the ground to build enough momentum for her feet to swing up toward its neck, and wrap herself around the robot, then executing submissive technique that brings Titanious to the floor under them as she locks its legs to her body. Hestius manages to pry the Titan's legs apart from one another with its hands, freeing his mech from her grasp, as it jerks its right leg away from her, and then the left. While Themis builds herself back up, Titanious hops onto the side of the reservoir, and dives toward her for an aerial elbow drop. However, Themis is just quick enough to stop the attack by driving the heel of her foot into the machine's chest, causing it to crash down beside her. The Titan proceeds to straddle her feet over the robot's body before grabbing it by the chest, and punching it in the face repeatedly. During this, Titanious grapples onto her once more, driving itself up to its feet before sweeping her fist away, and delivers a devastating headbutt.

Disoriented, Themis attempts to recompose herself, holding her head.

"You're stronger than I anticipated. Do you not fear death itself?"

Hestius gets in position with Titanious once more, and speaks through the mech's new external communication system, installed by Andy. "I died 2,500 years ago, yet here I am. Death is nothing to me now, and I will not let you stand in my way!"

The crimson goliath readies itself for a powerful cross, but as Titanious throws its right fist toward Themis, she swoops underneath it onto the top of her back, balanced on her hands, and performs a brutal kick to the mech's sternum with both her legs– a blow so powerful that the sheer force of it sends Titanious into the air. As the machine is airborne, Themis springs herself up before jumping to its level to deal a deadly knee drive to that same spot where she landed the kick. Titanious is absolutely defenseless at this point, so the Titan uses the reservoir walls to her advantage again, running along them, grabbing the red giant by its crown again before throwing it upward to gain more elevation. Themis continues this maddening juggle by pouncing side to side from the walls, and finishing her combo with a devastating flying uppercut that breaks them through the ceiling, and out to the surface of Argos, which had been evacuated due to a potential earthquake alert.

The two gargantuan behemoths enter the surface from the large hole created by Themis' uppercut– Titanious crashes into the city on its side, as its opponent lands gracefully on her feet, facing the mech with her arms crossed. The golden sun sets between them both.

"Is this really the best you can do?" she taunts before pointing to Titanious, as if to demean it and Hestius' skill. "I know you're holding back!"

Gritting his teeth, the frustrated Hestius' body glows bright orange once again. Titanious props itself back up to its feet with the same orange glow. The scarlet warrior turns itself to face Themis, illuminating further to the point where it looks as if the mech is bathing within the blazes of a supernova. As Hestius lets out a battle cry, the colossal machine aggressively positions itself into a fighting stance, bursting the fiery aura into a flurry of flames emitting from the red giant's chassis. Fotia Alpha is engaged.

"Is this what you want!?" shouts the demigod.

"That is more like it."

Themis draws a sword from its sheath within the backside of her armor, aiming her blade in the machine's direction with one arm, taking on a defensive stance. The two fighters slowly orbit one another, planning and preparing for their next moves. It is not long until they begin charging at one another with caution, with Titanious at a sprint, and Themis dragging her blade through the air with two hands. Once they get close just enough, the Titan slashes her sword upward, but only for the mech to tuck and roll away from the attack, and position itself for a tackle, to which it executes. The very metal the machine is composed of, slowly begins to imprint itself onto its opponent, leaving her grunting at the burns of Fotia Alpha. The moment before they both collapse onto the ground beneath them, Themis, with her quick wit, immediately grabs onto the crimson goliath, and manages to catch herself with her feet, leading to a snap down, causing Titanious to get slammed underneath her. The Titan scurries away from the intense heat before lunging her body towards the red giant for a jab with her sword, in hopes to penetrate the seams of its armor. But, Titanious shifts away from the strike, to which Themis uses her momentum from her blade getting stuck to the ground to perform a swinging kick to the machine's chest, successfully knocking him backwards. As the mech rolls back into a kneeling position, the blade of Themis swings downward upon on, leaving it no choice but to defend itself with its arms, rendering her attack useless. Themis presses on, driving the force of her weight and weapon to move her opponent backwards. However, this only makes the fire of Hestius burn brighter, as the flames of Fotia Alpha grow more intense. Titanious steps back up to its feet, and breaks away his guard to open the Titan up for an attack. At this moment, the fists of the scarlet warrior turn inferno red. With Hestius crying out once more, Titanious gathers his momentum to unleash the explosive power of the Titan Buster to Themis' body– the impact resulting into a massive, concentrated pyrokinetic blast, which sends the opponent flying backwards across several blocks.

Collapsing against the side of a building, the Titan uses her sword to carry herself back up, as the mech marches toward her, engulfed in flames. Themis assumes a defensive position once more, eyeing Titanious as it treads forth. She takes several breaths to relax herself, repositioning her blade for another strike. Shortly after, the Titan begins to release a battle cry of her own before charging towards the fiery mech, and unleashes a series of slashes with her sword at it, to which Titanious blocks and parries every single one with its cratonium arms. Despite this, Themis presses on– the attacks become quicker, more intense, violent. Desperate. She has full intentions of killing her enemy until her last breath. But as one of her swipes comes from above, Titanious moves slightly to its right, rotating as it lays its hands onto the Titan, and uses her momentum to send her flying forward. Thankfully, she manages to maneuver while airborne to face the mech as she lands onto her feet, catching herself by driving her blade into the ground.

As she recollects her energy, Themis takes on another stance, only this time, the burning Titanious follows suit, and the two stare down on another. Seconds pass, but it is as if time stands still between them, as the beams of the Greek sunset shine upon both fighters. Soon, the two warriors exert their breaths and vocal chords to shout at one another before they both commit to a full on sprint. They build up more and more momentum as they charge at one another, with Themis readying her blade for impact. She is ready to finally execute her opponent once and for all. At the exact second the two giants pass by one another, the Titan slashes her sword at the machine's midsection, and the two remain still. Themis exhales profusely from expending so much of her energy, all while Titanious seemingly powers down, as its flames fade away into nothingness. But little does she realize, Hestius is still breathing. In fact, her sword has failed to strike Titanious, as a large piece of her blade had snapped away upon impact, as it finally comes down from the heavens, and pierces itself into the ground. The mech has simply reverted back to base form, and is still active.

"No…" Themis tells herself in disbelief before collapsing onto her knees, with her shattered sword in her hands.

Hestius moves Titanious to face its opponent, but with a hint of sorrow before walking towards her.

Themis peers back behind her with a defeated expression. "Do what you must. I have failed, and I'm no longer of any use."

Titanious stops in its tracks. Hestius, after catching his breath, speaks to her through the mech's comm system. "And what makes you believe that?"

The Titan turns her head away, gazing down upon her broken blade. "I am your enemy, and I have lost. You must destroy me, like how I've tried to destroy you. You said you wouldn't let me stand in your way, did you not?"

"I did. And now you are no longer in my way."

She scoffs. "And what makes you think that I won't turn around and end your life with this blade of mine?"

"Because there is nothing you can do right now. You fought me knowing your weapon could not penetrate my cratonium alloy. So tell me again… why should I finish you right here and now?"

Themis lowers her head for another several inches, pausing.

"You said you wanted to destroy me, and me only. You captured my friend, knowing I would make myself vulnerable to save him. You chose to spy on me, instead of attacking me from the start. This only tells me that you did not want to put other lives at risk."

"Yes… because it isn't fair… No one else should have to suffer for my means."

"So you are still true to yourself in some way."

She sighs. "Please stop the lecturing and just kill me already."

Titanious stares down at Themis before deciding to walk past her.

"I will give you this chance to walk away from this war. Under the condition that you promise me one thing, and one thing only."

The Titan slowly looks to the crimson goliath.

Titanious turns to face her. "Promise me that you will live. I know this is a cause you did not join willingly."

"… Thanks." Themis begins to prop herself back onto her feet, and faces the mech. "But my life is nothing to you, nor should it be. Whatever happens to me is none of your concern. I shall remove myself from the alliance if I must, but if you dare try and interfere with my defiance, I will not hesitate to finish what I started, and for good."

Hestius takes in her harsh response. "I understand."

"And so you know, Ares never sent me to kill you. You will see why soon enough, for I do not owe you an explanation. I will abide by your request, but only as long as I never see you again. There is no telling what will happen."

The two giants face one another, as if to give silent goodbyes before Themis proceeds to walk off toward the descending sun on the horizon. Hestius watches on.

Back at the castle ruins, Andy sits against the stone wall behind him, watching the night sky as his torso is still bound in rope, having already freed his mouth after constant squirming. The young man perks his head to the side a little, hearing a faint, yet familiar synthetic hum as it approaches. Hestius enters with Crimson Magma, parking it before stepping off to release his friend from being tied up.

"Heh. Took you long enough." Andy remarks.

"You wanted me to leave you behind, correct?" Hestius kneels down, undoing the rope to let his arms loose.

"Yeah, well, I changed my mind the second you bailed."

"Well, the good thing is you were not harmed." The demigod tosses the rope aside.

Andy rolls his shoulders around to get some blood flow going, and looks at Hestius. "Appreciate it, regardless."

The redhead decides to take a seat right next to him, watching the stars above. "I decided to let her go."

Andy turns his head at him. "Oh yeah?"

"I had a feeling that she did not join the alliance by choice. She told me she wanted to kill me on her own accord, and not on Ares' orders. She never told me why, yet insisted that I would find out soon enough. She went after me, knowing both what I was capable of, and that she would fail... It really makes you wonder."

"And she also said something along the lines of not hesitating to kill you if she had the chance?"

"Yes... Yes, she did." Hestius pauses, and faces Andy. "How did you know?"

The demigod's partner gives a small chuckle. "I heard everything, dude. And... I'm sorry, but you sound like you're in love with her."

"W-What?" blushes Hestius.

"Oh, Themis. Promise me. Promise me that you will live." mocks Andy, bursting in laughter.

The redhead grows even more red. "Stop! It is not like that!"

"Oh, Hestius, you are so kind, but I'm still going to kill you."

"Knock it off! I mean it!"

The young man continues to cackle. "Such a way with words. Did you learn that from your mom, or your dad?"

Hestius tries to hide his face with one of his hands, still pink and annoyed "N-Neither, I was just being honest!"

"Chill man, I'm just joshin' ya." Andy relaxes, catching a breath.

The two stare back up at the dark sky once more, as the moon beams rain upon them.

CHAPTER VIII: RAGE

Deep in the hellish depths of Tartarus, the Titan king Kronos marches down the throneroom of Ares. At his side, a woman bearing similar creaturesque features and armor– the wife of Kronos, the queen of the Titans, Rheia. They both stroll toward their master, who awaits them on his throne. Ares stares down upon the two Titans as they kneel before him.

"The mission, sire." speaks Kronos.

"Themis has defected, and abandoned the alliance." adds Rheia.

The god of war stays fixated on the two giants. Air is pushed roughly from his nostrils.

The Titan king calls out. "What shall we do next, my lord?"

Ares remains still for another brief moment. "How are the experiments coming along?"

"Well, sire… we have discovered something with the current trial." Rheia answers. "We advise that you come and see it for yourself"

"Is that so?" the war god rises from his throne.

The three search for the arena where these so-called experiments have been conducted. The Titans and god find Mnemosyne, the Titan of memory, who watches over the arena, which has been sealed within a dome composed of souls, in place to hold an erratic multi-headed dragon, its deafening cries echoing through the chambers.

"Mnemosyne." Ares calls.

The Titan, clad in black feathers, shifts her serpentine focus to him before kneeling. "My liege."

"The trial is going smoothly, I presume?"

"Yes, indeed." she rises. "The armor you had brought here long ago, after further examination, carries the essence of a powerful creature who had once roamed before– with power unlike any other."

"... Typhon…"

"It appears that in the face of death, its body was reforged into this very armor."

"Interesting… and the Hydra?"

"Typhon and the Hydra share the same genetic make-up– it is its offspring. And once we had merged the armor with the Hydra… it completely rebuilt its body."

The now bio-cybernetic behemoth flails about, spewing a poisonous gas before summoning a gold aura around its body before releasing a discharge of electricity from its maws inside its deathly prison, creating an explosion that ends up damaging itself. Escape is futile, but the cybernetic properties of the Hydra proceed to self-repair.

"And as you can see, its behavior is violent. Even more than before death. I have tried to keep it in control, but nothing seems to work. It is as if it only gets angrier."

Ares looks down at the rageful hybrid. "And what do you suggest it needs in order for it to be ready?"

"An intellect. Without it, the Hydra is still nothing but a mindless creature."

"The armor… would you say it *bonded* with it?"

"Symbiotically… Though, I am afraid we are seeing no further progress." Mnemosyne lowers her head in shame. "I am sorry, my lord. As much as I would hate to start from scratch, we can use this information for future experiments! I will look further into the souls of the beasts that have fallen during the war–"

"No need." affirms Ares. "... Open the arena."

"Y-Yes, sire." she stammers.

Mnemosyne releases the souls. The smoke and poisonous gas ascends into the black clouds of Tartarus, uncovering the mechanized monster. The Hydra looks over to the war god and three Titans, but comes to a freeze upon recognizing Ares. Ares steps forth into the arena, leaving the beast to cower back, yet snarl.

"Come forth, Mnemosyne." he commands.

Mnemosyne slowly treads toward Ares before standing at his side.

"You see… the beast may be belligerent, but it still knows fear when faced with it."

"You mean…" Mnmosyne looks to the Hydra, and then to him. "… is it likely to obey orders?"

"It will do anything to survive. That is what I am counting on." Ares rests his hand on her shoulder. "But let us be sure of it."

The war god swiftly pulls her by the wrist, and comes toward the beast.

"Wait! Stop! What are you doing!?" Mnemosyne cries. Each plea for a reason grows more desperate as they inch closer to the biosynthetic behemoth. It gets to a point where she tries fighting back, and attempts to pull in the opposite direction, but to no avail. "What is the meaning of this my lord!?" Tears begin to erupt from her eyes, as she approaches an unknown fate.

Ares drags Mnemosyne's helpless body, as his presence forces the creature to bow before him. The god of war then walks upon the creature, and in an instant, forces the Titan's body into the source in which the Hydra's assimilation had sprouted, as Kronos and Rheia look on through sheer curiosity. It is not long until the Hydra and Mnemosyne become a singular entity.

Several days pass as an intense thunderstorm takes Greece and its neighboring islands, following one of the most vicious storms ever recorded for the country for how long it has persisted on and off. The ocean waves grow more furious as they crash onto Keros Island, with massive winds piercing through. Hades has the electricity shut off in the house, opting to light a series of small candles throughout. However, this does not apply to Andy, who is showing Hestius how to play *Super Street Fighter II: Turbo* in their chambers, maining Chun-Li, as the demigod learns through Blanka. The death god marches up the stairs, candle in one hand, to the sounds of spinning bird kicks and various roll attacks, and enters the young mens' room.

"I suggest that the two of you stop the game for now." Hades commands.

Hestius pauses the game midway through the match.

"Hey!" shouts Andy. "What gives?"

"Hades asked us to stop playing."

"In times like these, I wish to reduce the use of electricity." adds Hades.

"What, are you paying rent to someone?" questions Andy.

"Do you think I built this house myself? Even immortals must pay their dues."

"Hold on a second, you're telling me you have a mortgage!?"

"Is there something unordinary about that? However, the property is fully paid for. I just take care of bills now."

Andy attempts to gather a whole scramble of thoughts coursing through his head in the moment. "H-How the hell does that work? Do you even have a job!?"

"When you have lived through entire centuries, you are bound to find ways to grow your wealth. Perhaps a genius such as yourself can learn a thing or two through energy conservation. I will ask again that you shut the game off."

Andy lets out a defeated sigh. "Alright…" Suddenly, something sparks within him. "But, just so you know, uh… I was showing Hestius here some, uh, stuff he can do to help his fighting capabilities with Titanious." He starts to grow more tense in his painfully obvious lie. "D-Do you mind if we just play one more game?"

Hades stares down the two as if they are thieves. Thieves of energy that is going to waste, and would increase the electricity bill. "One more game." he says before leaving them be.

Andy now releases a deep exhale in relief before urging Hestius to unpause their game.

"That was quite a bold strategy, Andy." Hestius remarks, performing his character's electric abilities.

"Eh, I mean, I'm sure there's something you can take away from this."

Hades sits within the living room in isolation, sitting at the center of the couch to himself, upright, but lost in thought with his head down, speaking to himself.

"This storm has lasted for days… it does not seem right. Have I gone mad? Paranoid? Surely things like this happen. They must."

The elderly god fixates his vision towards the ceiling, looking to the heavens.

"Zeus, my brother… You would know, would you not? … If only I could see you again. But perhaps, you may not welcome such a reunion. Though, I do not blame you for growing bitter. Not after everything this world had seen."

Hades then faces the television screen before, peering into its black void.

"… But one thing I do know… is you must always question your intuition."

He swiftly swipes the remote from his side to power on the TV before him. A news broadcast covering the storm in Thessaloniki runs through. Apparently, it is where the storm has been the most dangerous, with flooding and debris running rampant. However, lightning strikes are more prevalent, further explaining the chaos within the city. Hades becomes laser-focused on the broadcast, yet, something catches his attention: whenever the thunder clouds crack, a silhouette appears. Judging by the distance of the cloud, and the light illuminating it, whatever is hiding in the sky must be another colossal creature.

"How can this be…? I knew I had sensed something… but why was I not sure? No… this feeling… it cannot be."

A demented possibility has shaken the god of the dead to his core– one of his souls was tampered with, and is now unleashed onto Earth for evil.

Upstairs, the demigod has bested his intelligent ally in virtual combat.

"Hey, no fair!" cries Andy. "All you did was spam your rolling attacks!"

Hestius, confused, replies. "Then why did the game allow me to do it as such? Is there a rule saying I should not?"

"Sportsmanlike conduct, man! You don't just kick a man while he's down! Where's your honor?"

"I mean, it is only just a game, correct? Is it not just for fun?"

"Yeah, but not when you're being a dirty cheat!"

"I cheated?"

"Ye– no! I mean, you, uh, hng." Andy desperately stammers, visibly upset over losing, while also trying to explain the ethics of playing tournament fighters to someone who has clearly never played a video game in his life.

"Gentlemen." Hades calls as he enters the room once more.

Andy jumps in his seat, shifting to Hades, even more tense than before. "W-Woah! Hades! I swear, we are *just* finishing up!"

"Good. Because for the first time in 2,500 years… I have felt fear."

"Hades?" Hestius looks at the elderly god with concern. "What do you mean by this?"

All three of them gather in the living room in front of the TV, letting the weather forecast in Thessaloniki run through.

"There." Hades points to the same silhouette he saw before.

Hestius and Andy take a closer look into the screen, eyeing the cloud as lightning courses through it.

"An aircraft?" Hestius asks.

"Guess whoever's flying it didn't get the memo." Andy suggests.

"Not an aircraft. And definitely not of this world." Hades affirms.

Hestius shifts his focus to Hades with a slight shock. "You mean it's–"

"A UFO?" Andy questions.

"Lately, I've had this feeling in my soul. This dread that something was not right, yet here it is, under my nose this entire time." The god of the dead slowly paces around the room.

"Not to be rude, but what exactly has gotten you worked up?" asks Andy.

"Please explain." demands Hestius.

Hades turns to them. "What you see in that broadcast is an undead creature."

"You mean like a zombie?" Andy scratches his head. "Isn't that your thing, or something?"

"When I served under Ares during the war, I demonstrated the potential of my necromantic powers to prove myself worthy of providing manpower to his cause. I summoned millions upon millions of souls, including that of monsters." he slowly approaches the two young men. "It appears that Ares himself had learned the ways of necromancy to strengthen his forces– to create troops from my own power."

"What!?" shouts Hestius. "But how!?"

"My only guess is that Mnemosyne helped him achieve such a power, for she possesses a great intellect amongst the Titans."

"But you know what this means, do you? Ares can grow his army a thousandfold at his own will now!"

"This is true… But I sense that it is not true necromancy, for I could not quite sense this being's presence. I suspect it was not a complete revival from death– for death still lingers within it. An old life was indeed summoned, though not in the ways of sorcery, but something more… cryptic. Neither man-made, or mystic."

Andy sits down quietly, crossing his arms, facing nothing. "So first, we've dealt with monsters, and now zombies are in the mix. Yet, somehow, we've jumped straight to monster zombies that might not even be real zombies, and can fly, create thunderstorms, and possibly level entire cities… Yeah, I'm thinking it's the end times, alright."

"Do not lie in the shadow of defeat, boy." Hades requests Andy, clenching a fist. "If this thing has died before, it can damn well die again."

Hestius swiftly turns away. "I will get Titanious ready."

"Hey, wait a sec!" calls Andy. "We don't even know how to get to this thing, and last I checked, you can't even fly!"

"The boy is correct, Hestius. We have to plan carefully if you wish to take on this beast alone."

Hestius pauses with grit for a brief moment. Slowly, he retreats back to them. "Apologies for my rashness… Let us talk this through."

Andy leans back to think over a plan. "OTE Tower is the largest building in Thessaloniki at about 80 meters, but it looks like the creature is a good 2,000, give or take.

So that's a no-go. Besides, you can't even touch it without it crumbling."

"What about any mountain regions? Could they be of any use?" Hestius asks.

"Well…" Andy pauses. "You have Mount Chortiatis, which peaks at over 1,200 meters, and Olympus at nearly 3,000. Only problem is that they're a pretty good way from the city, so using them won't be of any good use, with Chortiatis being around 30 kilometers away, and 90 for Olympus."

Hestius strokes his chin to think of any other strategies, but proceeds to recall his uses of the Titan Buster– specifically, the one from his battle with Themis, and how it had blasted her across Argos. The massive combustible blasts from the fists of the vermilion knight spark a light in the demigod's head. "Actually…" he says to Andy. "Something tells me they would."

"What do you got?" Andy looks to Hestius with anticipation.

"Titanious responds to my emotions and will, which allows it to increase its power… I am thinking that if I power up to Fotia Alpha, I could use the Titan Buster to launch myself toward the enemy."

"You might be onto something… But do you know for sure that the Titan Buster is that strong?"

"Not entirely certain, but when I used it against Themis, she was launched a good distance… I want to say about 700 meters. Granted, she was lighter, but I think if I can concentrate enough of Titanious' power, I can possibly reach it."

Andy rubs his temples to focus. "So let's say you can probably get yourself at least 500 meters off the ground… It's still not enough to even make half of that…." Suddenly, his eyes widened a small bit after thinking it over. "But if we get a running start, build up some momentum, we can probably push it. Maybe not 2,000, but we can maybe get something…."

Hestius cocks an eyebrow at Andy. "What exactly do you have in mind…?"

Time passes as the storm grows stronger, more fierce. Thunder cracks the Earth as the demigod approaches the southeast side of Mount Chortiatis with Titanious before climbing up the terrain. He reaches the top, and in the distance, the anomalous storm clouds lie ahead.

"Andy, I see it." Hestius speaks into comms.

"Alright, now that we've pinpointed it, let's get this party started. What's it looking like? The weather is jamming the radar. Cameras are all fuzzy, too"

"The creature is still hiding in the clouds." the demigod assesses. He looks to the grounds of Thessaloniki, and notices a path that the beast in the sky is creating with the storm. "Andy, I think it is moving deeper into the city. I will need to cover more distance than anticipated."

"Well, we better do something quick, because the longer we sit and think, the more this plan is gonna cost us!"

The demigod stares back up at the dark clouds, as if to analyze them.

"Hey, Hes, what's the deal?"

"It does not know I am here… I should try drawing its attention. That way, I can shorten the distance."

"Well, act fast, or we're gonna lose it!"

The redhead uses Titanious to scan its surroundings. A few seconds go by before a series of radio towers make their presence in the vicinity. Several of the towers have been damaged from the lightning strikes, with sparks spewing from their transformers. The mech proceeds to slide down the mountain toward the towers, and tears one of them out from the ground, pulling its cables and connectors apart. Grasping the metallic monolith, the red giant traverses back up to the mountain's peak. Hestius eyes his target, and carefully examines the foggy mass before raising the large steel apparatus in front of the mech. Titanious then crushes the tower in its hand, and uses the other to help reshape it into the form of a javelin. The vermilion knight then winds back its arm with the spear, and raises the opposite.

Hestius takes a breath, shutting his eyelids.

"You have taken me this far… Do the same for my power."

The demigod releases his vision with an exhale, and uses as much force as possible to launch the radio tower javelin with all of Titanious' might. The spear slices through the air, flying toward the clouds, before it gets lost in the mass of lightning emitting from it.

Suddenly, the thunder stops. The clouds begin to gradually reform.

"Andy, it is coming my way!"

"Good, now move it!"

Titanious turns away, and proceeds to roll down the side of Mount Chortiatis it came, gathering as much speed as possible to reach its starting point before tumbling down to the base, and crawling to a sprint to the location. The creature in the clouds slithers slowly through the sky to approach the mountain as the scarlet warrior pushes on until finally reaching the point. Hestius grits his teeth and handles the controls of Titanious with a death grip, beginning to initiate that orange glow that would fuel the machine's power. Crying out to the storm with a furious scream, Titanious powers up to Fotia Alpha before pivoting off the starting point, and begins to sprint towards the mountainside.

"Andy, Fotia Alpha is powered up!"

"Alright, you know what to do."

The burning red mech charges on, digging its feet into the surface beneath, and driving its elbows back to slice the raging wind for more acceleration. The flames of Titanious burn brighter as Hestius forces the controls to keep striding, his heart beating faster, pumping more blood to power it up. The machine leaves a blazing trail, getting closer to the base of Mount Chortiatis with more speed.

"Launching now!" the demigod shouts. Titanious dives toward the bottom of the mountain, embers coursing through its body, and down its arms. The mech lands onto the palms of its hands as the rest of its body maneuvers over. Shortly, a concentrated blast from Titanious' fists combust into ground, and fires the red giant up the mountain. As the machine soars up Mount Chortiatis, rolls itself forward to perform another blast at about 500 meters up. Concentrating its energy into another use of the Titan Buster, more momentum is gained– the additional push has elevated Titanious faster than before, causing it to flip through the air at tremendous speed. All that is left is one more blast at the top of the mountain. Hestius tries to focus on Mount Chortiatis' peak, and submerges his mind into tunnel vision– there is only him and the mountaintop. He cannot afford to miss the timing of this last shot. 800 meters, 900 meters, 1,000 meters. Titanious flies closer, as the window shrinks.

1,025… 1,050… 1,075… 1,100…

"Guide my power once more."

1,140… 1,150… 1,160…

Hestius prepares Titanious for another launch.

1,170… 1,180… 1,190…

Shifting the raw power of Fotia Alpha to the gauntlets of the red giant, until finally, after reaching the peak of the mountain, another explosive blast is discharged, launching the vermilion knight towards the heavens, as it now accumulates more height, overcoming Mount Chortiatis' 1,200 meter elevation, and pushing towards

1,500– eventually, 1,800– and even suprasses to 2,200 meters.

Now, the crimson mech enters the clouds. The momentum accumulated from the blast begins to wane, as Titanious begins to fall back towards the Earth, still ablaze, traversing through the thick mass of fog in the sky, electricity flowing through the creases. Though, it is not long until the machine finds itself in a clear zone within. But in the distance, a part-mechanical multi-headed dragon whose body stretches on for about the size of a naval warship. The newly reborn Hydra terrorizes the city of Thessaloniki.

"What...? What is this!?"

Hestius becomes stunned at the sight of the monster, as it is facing his direction, each of its heads releasing a deafening shriek at the demigod's presence.

One of the beast's organic heads throws itself towards the flaming red giant, and traps it within its teeth. Titanious, caught in the clenches of the creature's mouth, attempts to pry itself out before resorting to punching the head repeatedly as they swim through the air. Thankfully, Hestius manages to build up just enough energy to release another blast from the Titan Buster, successfully destroying the Hydra head, the impact leading to another free fall. Out comes another one of its heads– this one tries to bite at Titanious, but falls to a short delay in its execution, as the fiery mech uses its hands to keep the jaws of the monster wide open. The two proceed to flail about in the sky, right up until one of the Hydra's metallic heads comes forth, and begins to glow yellow, charging up something within. Upon reflex, the blazing vermilion knight pounces off the dragon's maw at the very second an electric charge blasts the head into an explosion.

Titanious crashes onto the body of the metallic mass, Hestius analyzes the dismembered heads of his enemy, only to see that a sort of mechanical matter sprouts from each of the necks, slowly reforming new heads,

"No… It cannot be!"

The reality that the Hydra has returned settles within the depths of the demigod's soul. Suddenly, the voice of Andy comes out from his communication system.

"Hes! Sorry for calling so late– guess we just went through a dead zone. Radar and cameras are back on, and *just what the hell is this!?"*

"Ares has brought the Hydra back to life!"

"Wait, seriously!? *The* Hydra!?"

"Indeed." Hestius props Titanious back to its feet, looking at the many heads of the mecha Hydra as they swoop around and about, all while two newly reformed cybernetic heads replace each of the necks that were destroyed. "It has some sort of metal tissue surrounding its body, and it is using it to heal itself!"

"Oh, jeez. Any idea what to do?"

As the heads of the Hydra stalk around Titanious, the mech takes a stance, facing them until a figure enters his peripheral. Hestius shifts his attention to what appears to be a torso that has been infused in the back of the Hydra. His eyes grow wider.

"Mnemosyne!?"

Mnemosyne's upper body is hunched over, but slowly rises upward as she awakens. She reaches toward the crimson mech, still in Fotia Alpha.

"Please… save me." She quietly begs.

The demigod stares at the horrific apparatus. "What have they done to you…!?"

A strange, dark voice echoes through the clouds.

"We have waited for you, young Hestius."

The redhead quickly checks his surroundings, and at the floating mass of dragon heads that circle him. Shortly, a large, full-body apparition of Ares, clad in his horned armor, appears in the clouds.

"Ares…" the demigod calls to the figure's presence. "What have you done!?"

"I have merely conducted a test for your very being. It is unfortunate that we could not meet face-to-face. Yet, in time, our fated reunion will come. But know this, destiny will arrive… And it all starts with you."

Mnemosyne proceeds to let out a weak cry. "Boy…"

The flaming Titanious turns back to her direction.

The voice of the god of war comes again.

"Victory will not be as simple as you think. In order to put a stop to this attack, you must put Mnemosyne out of her misery, ending her pain and suffering. But her lifeforce flows within the blood of the Hydra– and this creature, at the will of my doing, shall do anything to survive."

The fires on the crimson mech burn slightly brighter.

"You monster…" Hestius utters in frustration. "What is it you wish to gain from this twisted plan of yours!? What exactly warrants this– this cruelty from whatever demented necromancy you performed!?"

"Oh, child… What you see before you is a small taste of the power you have sought since your youth. The question is… are you worthy enough to achieve it?"

"Enough with the mind games! What are you getting at!?"

"You shall see soon enough... Though, since we are now calling this a game, let us begin."

As the ghastly image of Ares evaporates, several of the Mnemosyne Hydra's organic heads let out that same ear-piercing shriek from before– each one proceeds to strike at the flaming Titanious, who manages to dodge them as they come.

"Yo, Hes." Andy calls into comms. "The hell was that?"

"Ares. I do not know what he is scheming, but if he wants to test my power, I will show him the *true* power of Titanious!"

Hestius grunts while evading the Mnemosyne Hydra's heads, blocking them off with the abilities of Fotia Alpha, using the Titan Buster at any given moment, but only to deflect their attacks, all while the fires illuminating the mech grow more intense. It is not long until the Mnemosyne Hydra's cybernetic heads start to burst lightning at the burning machine while it tries desperately to duck away from them and the other serpentine necks.

"Hes, behind you!" Shouts Andy in comms.

In the midst of all the dodging, Titanious is eventually blindsided by one of the electric blasts that hits it in the back, knocking it a good distance along the Mnemosyne Hydra's body, and away from where Mnemosyne is held. As the blazing mech starts to recover, one of the organic heads releases its poisonous gas within the vicinity, as the green mass surrounds Titanious.

"What is this, gas?" Andy questions.

"It is the Hydra's poison." Hestius looks around to examine.

"That's… fine, right? I mean, you're practically invincible in there after all."

"I should be– cratonium is impenetrable."

The embers of Titanious glow further, but as the emerald fog covers the mech, they begin to diminish. Right away, Hestius lets out a small groan.

"Yo, Hes, what's going on?"

"Suddenly, I feel strange… as if I am getting fatigued."

"Fatigued? Could it be the poison?"

"That… And the connection I have with Titanious. It is trying to sever it!"

As the flames of the scarlet warrior shrink, it proceeds to sprint to Mnemosyne's location.

"To your right!"

Shortly, one of the Hydra's organic heads pop up from the mist, to which Titanious retaliates with a desperate execution from the Titan Buster. However, upon impact, the attack ignites the entire cloud of gas into a massive explosion. The detonation launches the mech through its blazes, as fire is set scattered across the creature's back. Moments after crashing, a metallic head sprouts toward Titanious, who uses its hands to stop its charge. The vermilion knight uses its leverage to push itself back up to its feet, but unfortunately, the scorching aura Titanious once had now disappears.

"No!" Hestius shouts in disbelief, slightly disoriented.

"Titanious' temperature just decreased– what's going on!?"

"The gas… it powered it down!"

The mechanical dragon head swoops downward and swipes the mech away, and sends itself towards it, clenching its jaws down onto the machine's midsection, squeezing it. Titanious struggles to break free from its grasp. But as Hestius, with all of his nauseous might, attempts to pry himself out, the teeth of the mecha Hydra pierce through the hull, leaving the demigod in shock.

"What!? How!?"

Sparks spout from the red giant's chassis before transitioning to flames once more, granting Titanious the strength to perform another Titan Buster to dislodge itself from the creature's mouth, leaving it to scurry away.

"Andy, the alloy of this beast– it's cratonium!"

"Seriously? How's that even possible!?"

"I do not know, but it is capable of restoring itself. It has been repairing whatever heads I destroy. I have never seen it do this before– it is as if the alloy has a mind of its own!"

"Can you count how many heads there are?"

Hestius looks around as Titanious is in Fotia Alpha again, eyeing the Mnemosyne Hydra heads that stalk around him.

"Right now, I see sixteen. Two of them are still natural."

"Good, cause I have an idea."

"Save it for now."

Two more heads lunge out to attack the scorching mech, Hestius doing what he can to steer from each strike. Titanious then finds itself on the run towards Mnemosyne again.

"Alright, what is it, Andy?"

"When you used the Titan Buster inside the gas cloud, it ignited. I'm thinking that if we use it while one of the heads is releasing it, we cause a chain reaction that can do some serious damage to it from the inside."

"Sounds like a good plan. Only problem is that I will power down again."

"Well, it's worth a shot. And I suggest you book it to Mnemosyne as soon as you do it. You're already outmatched as it is"

One of the Mnemosyne Hydra's organic heads comes about once more, and chases Titanious.

"Perfect!" shouts Andy. "We just gotta wait for the right moment."

The crimson mech presses on, and the serpentine head slithers and sweeps over and around it before releasing its gas directly at it.

"Jackpot." Andy affirms.

Titanious charges its right fist, and hurls it into the mouth of the creature, which causes another massive explosion– but only this time, the body of the Mnemosyne Hydra begins to tremble like an earthquake. Smoke shrouds the entire aerial battlefield.

"Well, that did it. Now go!" Andy commands.

Titanious starts sprinting again, but with a sluggish demeanor.

"How are you holding up?"

Hestius coughs. "It worked… I just need to regain my stamina."

"Hang in there, the camera's getting fuzzy again from all the haze, but your radar should tell you there's something just up ahea–"

As soon as Titanious is about to reach the body of Mnemosyne, another one of the mechanical heads burst out from the smoke, and immediately shoots an electric beam, which lands as a direct hit to the red giant, firing it backwards, tumbling down the creature's body. As Titanious begins to recover, two more mechanical heads show up, and pin both of its arms down with their jaws. The mech fights to push forward, but the struggle of cratonium against cratonium is proven futile as the teeth dig into Titanious' armored plating and circuitry, rendering it completely defenseless. Soon enough, the last organic head of the beast hovers forth, and releases its gas, as if to taunt the machine. This weakens the mech further. Hestius cries out with his might, as if screaming would get Titanious to function properly again. But as the organic head shifts away, another mechanical one descends upon the handiwork of its allied brethren, and charges up.

"Damn you…" curses Hestius.

The inside of the cybernetic dragon illuminates in amber, all while the demigod tries to escape the monster's grasp in distress.

"DAMN YOU ALL!!!" Tears erupt from his face, shining in sapphire.

A powerful blast of electricity is discharged directly at Titanious through the green fog, resulting in another explosion that sets the sky ablaze. This one is larger than the previous, with shockwaves tearing through the air. The orange colossal fireball still remains– but inside of it, a small blue flame. A flame that grows bigger, while the explosion fades into smoke. Pieces of dismembered cybernetic dragon heads lay across the monster's back, as their serpentine roots slowly regenerate and duplicate. Finally, the smoke begins to clear. Titanious stands tall, now bathed in a blue fiery aura.

"ARES!!!" Hestius shouts into the sky as thunder cracks through the dark clouds. "IS THIS THE POWER YOU SPEAK OF!?"

"Hey, Hes!" Andy chimes in through comms. "What happened just now!?"

"Fotia Delta." Hestius replies. "That is what happened."

"For real!? I thought you were a goner!"

"Well, Andy, I am unsure how else to put it… but I am *really* pissed off right now."

"Oh, it's on, huh!?"

"You can bet your ass it is."

"Ha! Now you're speaking *my* language! Let's get these chumps!"

The remaining heads of the Mnemosyne Hydra slither and snarl at this sight beforing crying out a series of nasty bellows toward the towering mech.

The demigod sets his sights on the multitude of dragon heads, assuming a stance. "The end of your reign of terror starts here!"

The machine, burning in cobalt, charges into a dash– but, this time, Titanious appears to be moving with more grace, more swiftness in its sprint. The heads come barrelling toward its direction, only for the mech to throw both its arms down aside, and releases a set of blades from each gauntlet, composed of pure thermal energy, scorching in azure embers: the God Daggers. One of the mechanical heads tries to ram itself into Titanious, only for the fiery blue mech to pivot around, and decapitate the beast. Then comes another, to which Titanious executes a swift uppercut that slices the serpentine neck in half, up the middle, and through its skull. During this strike, another head attempts to sweep itself through the mech's lower body, only to get noticed by it, and is met with a blade driven into its forehead, and yanked out by Titanious, who proceeds to paint the entire battlefield with the blood of its fearsome opponent– beheading after beheading, severely decreasing the headcount of the beast, the brave warrior presses on. But as the final cybernetic head of the Mnemosyne Hydra charges its lightning attack, Titanious ducks under it just in time to avoid the attack, grab onto the monstrous head, and aim it towards the rest of the regenerating necks, further delaying their regeneration, as each one is struck by the constant pulse of electricity. The mech grips onto the head with both its arms, and proceeds to wrestle it down to the ground, and completely removes it from its nape. The machine then crushes and combusts the metallic dragon head with a dual Titan Buster before chucking it off into the distance.

With every one of the Mnemosyne Hydra's head being rid of its sight, Titanious charges back to Mnemosyne's body, which is slumped over in a dead position. The mech's feet skid to a stop before slowly approaching the Titan's torso protruding from the mechanical mass. Hestius looks toward Mnemosyne, and Mnemosyne slowly raises her head, fixating her painful eyes to the machine before her in its blazing blue glory. Titanious comes to a stop, facing the Titan before ascending its fiery right arm.

"Forgive me, Mnemosyne." Hestius speaks in a shimmer of remorse.

In an instant, the mech lunges toward the trapped body. However, an emerald glow emits from Mnemosyne's eyes– in a moment's notice, she proceeds to deflect Titanious' strike by swiping its right hand away with her left with cratonium gauntlets of her own, lacing her fingers around the machine's. To Hestius' shock, he quickly follows through by driving the flaming mass of a blade of the opposite arm towards her midsection. Unfortunately, the Titan manages to parry it all the same. Now the two have their hands locked together.

"Boy, you must listen very carefully." She alerts Hestius. "This body of mine… it is already dead. But I must warn you– you have to–"

Mnemosyne immediately starts to cry out in horror, as if the suffering she is enduring had only become excruciating. The demigod watches the Titan, and attempts to break free from her grasp, but Mnemosyne has an iron grip, rendering any chance of escape in the moment useless. Suddenly, Mnemosyne's once calm voice shifts to something more deathly… The Titan begins to scream. She screams as if the life from her body is being stripped away– like a lion skinning its prey alive.

"Mnemosyne!? What happened!?"

She says nothing. All she does is scream. But the screams start turning into roars– roars of fury and hatred.

Disgusted by this horror, the demigod, with Titanious burning brighter, persists in trying to release himself from the ghoulish grasp of Mnemosyne. The crimson goliath tightens its brace on her hands, as its azure fires grow more intense. Soon enough, as its grip becomes tighter, the vermilion knight's strength begins to outmatch that of the Titan's– and with a single push, Mnemosyne's wrists are pried open, causing her to release a deeply harrowing shriek, blood spilling from her arms, and out of the creases of her gauntlets.

"Whatever you are, the very moment your wretched soul finds its way to Tartarus, tell Ares I will not rest until I see the day where I destroy him!!!"

As the machine retracts its right arm, Hestius cries out victoriously, and runs its fiery blade through the heart of Mnemosyne. Titanious braces its left hand around the right gauntlet, and charges up a powerful and destructive Titan Buster. And shortly, the Titan is blown to smithereens. As smoke shrouds throughout the sky, Titanious remains triumphant once again. All seems to be done, but the battle has yet to finish.

"Well, Hes, you did it!" Andy celebrates.

"Yes, I did… Now how do I get down from here?" questions Hestius.

There is a sudden change in the wind. The very gravity on top of the Hydra's body feels to have shifted. Seconds after Mnemosyne was reduced to ash and blood, the aerial battlefield that is the creature's back begins to slowly plummet back down towards the Earth. Titanious tries to move about, but stumbles in an attempt to keep balance as the monster falls from the sky.

"It ain't gonna be easy…" warns Andy. "But I suggest you get off as quickly as possible– those heads should be coming back at any moment!"

"What do you mean? Destroying Mnemosyne was to halt the attack!"

"Half-true– it turns out she was what kept the Hydra afloat. You're gonna have to find its heart under all that armor."

"It is all cratonium, but the God Daggers can penetrate it."

"Oh yeah, that's another thing– you had *swords* this whole time!?"

"We will discuss this later!"

Titanious proceeds to drive one of its blades into the Hydra's body, and drags it along to make an opening. But before it could finish, the last organic head of the Hydra reappears, and pulls the flaming mech away before slamming it down, and slithers around it. The machine picks itself back up, and faces the serpentine head. The Hydra head charges at the red giant, who catches it by its muzzle, and slowly begins to force the creature's maw open with its two hands. Once the jaws are wide enough, Titanious stomps down to pin it, and drives itself further into the mouth, reaching with a single arm down its throat. Momentarily, the mech starts pulling at a large, fleshy orb until it completely severs it from the inside by sheer force– the apparatus is as a large sack, filled with what remains of the Hydra's poisonous gas. The momentum from such a great pluck causes Titanious to fall backwards, embracing the sack with its flaming metallic arms.

As the organic head scurries away in fear and tremendous pain from blood drizzling from its mouth, the machine props itself back up with its feet, with the poisonous pouch held to its chest. Titanious searches its surroundings at the newly formed mechanical mass of a total of thirty cybernetic dragon heads that now orbit around it. The scarlet warrior, doused in cerulean flames looks up and about at the metallic heads, as if to ponder. It then looks down at the sack within its grasp, searches for the opening it had made before, then turns its attention back to the Hydra's multitude of heads. One by one, the heads begin to hurl themselves toward Titanious' position. The machine leaps toward the Hydra's wound, takes the sack, and presses it down against the armored flooring beneath it. As the heads swim closer and closer through the air, the vermilion knight takes one of its God Daggers, and pierces it through the sack, followed by an instant Titan Buster– and at that moment, the entire creature is engulfed in a devastating, gargantuan explosion. Fire rains through the sky, as an inferno overtakes the clouds.

Out from the fiery mass from the explosion, a metallic figure is launched toward the heavens– it is Titanious, completely powered down to its base form, its flames extinguished. The chain reaction proceeds to disrupt the Hydra from the inside, as it crashes toward the Earth at a greater speed. In the course of all that, Hestius is knocked out, as anyone would be from such a concussive blast. Eyes closed to black, the ringing in his ears obscuring his senses– yet, there is a faint little voice that calls to the demigod.

"Hes, do you read me!? … Hes, are you there!? Hes!!!"

It is as if Hestius had inadvertently shaped his own fate– falling, like he once had 2,500 years ago. Suddenly, another voice appears, but in the echoes of his mind.

"Gabriel."

He awakens, finding himself in a free fall with Titanious.

"Do you read me, Hes!"

"Loud and clear, Andy."

"Oh, thank God, are you good, man!?"

"I think so… But by the looks of it, my little stunt may result in catastrophic damage."

"Got any ideas?"

The demigod thinks to himself, watching the large creature descend further and further. "... I may have one in mind."

Titanious narrows itself to accumulate momentum, closing the distance to the Hydra, covered in bursting flames. Hestius further analyzes its target during the dive, seeing through the smokey conflagration.

"I see it!" Just below the demigod, and in the midst of the Hydra's destruction, a gigantic, pulsating green mass of tissue. "I see the Hydra's heart– it still beats!"

"You mean it's still alive!?"

"Indeed. But I know how to take care of it."

Titanious powers up to Fotia Alpha, and curls itself upward to change position. Now, instead of diving, the mech extends its legs, and leads with its feet. Slowly, the blazing red giant elevates its right knee, and raises both its arms upward, clasping both hands together. Titanious slowly adjusts itself in the air to find its trajectory, until it finds itself directly on top of the still-beating heart.

"This… is for you, Andy."

The mech now charges up to Fotia Delta, and proceeds to accumulate energy within its gauntlets. And all of a sudden, a powerful explosive discharge is released from the hands of Titanious– the Titan Buster has been initiated with tremendous might. The force of the blast accelerates the vermilion knight with incredible speed, getting closer and closer to the heart, building momentum from the fall. As he reaches the organ, Hestius hollers in a passionate affirmation that he will see victory to the end.

Seconds pass, and in an instant, Titanious kicks itself through the heart of the Hydra, completely obliterating it, all before the attack manages to drive the crimson machine through the creature's entire body, making a clean exit out of its underbelly. The surge of heat then causes yet another explosion– this time, the Hydra now bursts into a series of remains that fall from the sky like meteors.

Eventually, Titanious impacts the ground, touching back down to the Earth, but the amount of force accumulated from the fall and the attack results in a massive crater in the middle of an open field off the outskirts of Thessaloniki. But thankfully, the pieces of the now destroyed Hydra fall into and around it, reducing the damage that could have been done if Hestius had not performed such a deadly execution.

Dust fills the surrounding atmosphere, debris clattering left and right. The scarlet mech remains still in the large hole in the ground, hunched over on a single knee.

"Dude…" Andy calls. "That was sick!"

The demigod, in exhaustion, manages to crack an acute smile. "Indeed… We did it."

"No. *You* did it, man."

The demigod checks around himself to get a sense of his environment having returned to land. "Andy, can you give me a damage report?"

"Thankfully, whatever damage there is in Thessaloniki can be chalked up to just a bad lightning storm… followed by a sudden meteor shower that may have hit a couple fields, caused a big crater, but nothing too major."

"I see… I should be more cautious next time."

"Dude, I'm just pulling your leg! You did good– the city is saved, and no one's hurt as far as I can tell." Andy reassures. "By the way, you said the Hydra was made of cratonium, right?"

"Yes, I did."

"Do me a favor and grab as much as you can. It'll come in *real* handy for repairs."

"On it."

Titanious rises from the haze, as it begins to clear. The vermilion knight proceeds to tread within the crater, searching and scavenging pieces of the fallen Mnemosyne Hydra.

CHAPTER IX: PRIDE

A week has passed since the epic clash between Titanious and the Mnemosyne Hydra. Titan activity in Greece enters a period of silence, as the young warrior Hestius continues his training with Hades. The two engage in a bare-handed sparring match off the shore of Keros Island– the god of the dead hurls a left jab toward the demigod, who parries it away with his right arm, following it with a left hook. Realizing his torso is in the open, Hades bats away the incoming blow by charging his left knee across his body. Upon planting his foot back down into the sand, the dead god uses the momentum to generate force for a spin kick, swinging his right leg around to strike Hestius, who is quick enough to block the attack with his forearms before performing a series of kicks of his own, which are all deflected by Hades one by one. The demigod starts to become a little more greedy, and increases the intensity within his kicks– but the moment he fires his right heel towards the elderly god's face, Hades ducks under the attack, and leads an inside charge with a right uppercut. With no chance to defend himself in his current position, the demigod takes the blow to his gut, and uses it as a way to reestablish his stance by retaliating with a right hook to the god's side, which lands effectively, resulting in a grunt from both parties.

The two fighters back away from one another to catch air in their lungs with their hard breathing. Shortly, they regain their wind, and proceed to advance in their altercation– the two continue to exchange blows, while also evading and blocking each other's strikes. Soon, at the very moment the youngster and elder raise their right arms, they launch forward to execute a cross towards one another. And suddenly… stillness. The fists of both fighters stand a mere inch away from their target's faces, as the two pant heavily, staring into each other's eyes with slight competitive animosity. Slowly, they step away from each other once more.

"Well done." compliments Hades. "You have come a long way since we had begun."

Hestius collects his posture. "Thank you."

"Rest now. You have earned it."

The god of the dead turns away and retreats back to the island home as the demigod watches.

"One hell of a match, there!" Andy remarks. "I can tell your legs are getting better."

Hestius gives a slight smile to himself. "It does feel like yesterday when I had awakened from that mountain. I remember I could barely move."

"Hey, just be glad you could barely walk at all! … On top of being alive, of course." Andy gets a closer look at the demigod. "Say, you ever thought about getting a haircut?"

Hestius looks to him, then picks at one of his longer bangs, examining it. "I quite like this length, actually… It feels new, and I am fond of it."

"Gotcha, gotcha." Andy looks off to the plains of the island, then out to the sea. "Say, I was thinking about doing a little bit of camping tonight. Haven't really had the chance to do it in a while, and I figured it might be a good way to unwind– if you're down to join of course."

Hestius looks to his friend upon hearing the request. "Yes." he puts on a modest grin. "That would be nice."

Hades watches them from the window of his chambers, relaxed. The god of the dead slowly looks to his hand, as he proceeds to curl his fingers, as if to hold the hand of a long gone specter.

"If only you were here to see what your son has become… In a way, he makes me regret allowing you to embark toward the Elysian Plane, but he possesses every

one of your attributes. Your legacy still lives on, Gabriella. You should be proud."

Later in the evening, the two young men march their way through the plains of Keros Island. Stars scatter in the dark blue sky, as the moon beams down upon the stretch of land. On Andy's back, he carries a large pack full of snacks and utensils in addition to his sleeping bag. In contrast, Hestius grips onto the carrier for their tent, and another for their firewood in each hand respectively, with only his sleeping bag on his back.

"Alright." Andy plops his bag onto the ground beneath him. "I think this'll make for a good spot."

The two then get to work on assembling the stones and firewood. Andy searches around the inside of his bag, but with confusion.

"That's weird… I thought I had brought my lighter with me."

Meanwhile, Hestius kneels and reaches his hands into the stack of lumber and rocks they have piled together, and slowly seals his eyes shut.

"Come on, man, did I seriously leave it behind?" Andy scours further into his pack.

The demigod begins to glow a very subtle orange, keeping in contact with the wood.

Finally, Andy feels a cold prism in the depths of his bag, and pulls out the lighter he had been looking for with bright, wide eyes. "Hey, I found–!"

Instantaneously, a spark emerges from Hestius gripping onto one of the logs, which causes a fire to erupt. Andy watches, frozen in place, as the demigod stands back up, the glow fading away.

After the two had built their tents, and laid out their sleeping bags, Hestius and Andy are seated on near-opposite ends of their fire. The ally to the demigod plops a marshmallow onto a skewer, and passes it down to Hestius.

"Want one?" he asks.

Hestius looks at the white puff in slight confusion of its presence. Respectfully, he declines.

"No, thank you."

"All good." Andy suggests before putting his marshmallow into the fire.

The demigod remains fixated onto the flames before him, watching as the embers rise into the air, resting his arms on the top of his legs.

"Actually…" he says. "I'll take one with meat."

"Right on."

Andy continues to put together a s'more before taking some lamb meat, and skewers it. He then holds it out to Hestius, who grabs ahold of it, and raises it over the flame.

"You know…" says Andy. "I used to go on camping trips with my family before I moved over here… Every year was at a different spot, so it'd be more interesting. We'd go to Denver, Santa Fe, Seattle, and a whole bunch of other places. My dad didn't wanna pay for plane tickets, so we drove instead… Though, it was more adventurous that way."

Hestius eyes his food being swallowed by the fire. "Your family… How are they now?"

"They're, alright. Mom and dad call every week to check in on me. Sister's a little worried too, and she's getting ready to start high school next year. I don't blame her, though. We used to do everything together… Even if she'd threaten to sell off my collection if I didn't take her to the mall." he laughs.

The demigod removes his skewer from the fire, and starts to bite into it.

Andy settles a little more, watching Hestius.

"So… I realize you haven't exactly talked much about this, but what was your family like growing up?"

The redhead stops chewing.

"I-I'm sorry, I didn't mean to be rude. You don't have to answer that."

Hestius ingests. "... My family… Back then, I never really knew if I had one."

Andy watches him. "I mean, you had a mother and a father, right? Weren't they your family?"

"Indeed they were. But I was brought into this world and raised through, how do I say… peculiar circumstances."

"Oh… is that bad?"

"... I do not know… It is quite a lot to explain…"

"Hey, man, I don't mind. Again, you don't have to get into the thick of it if it's that bad."

"Well, that is the thing, Andy… My childhood was not bad."

"How do you mean…?"

Hestius takes a deep breath before continuing to stare into the fire. "My father Hephaestus and the goddess Aphrodite were in love… but as Ares began his rise as an expert military strategist, Aphrodite grew more supportive of him, instead."

"Let me guess… she got *too* supportive."

"You can say that. This left a pit in my father's soul. For some time, he would wander the Earth, where he would then find interest in a human: my mother… From what I know, they were happy with one another. They wanted me in this world… but for a god and a human to form such a bond was forbidden– unless you were Zeus."

"Ah, figures." Andy sips on some cola.

"My father made an agreement with my mother and Aphrodite. I was given the name Hestius, son of Hephaestus and Aphrodite, and named after the righteous Hestia. This was so I could live amongst the gods, so they would not know that I carried mortal blood within me."

"How did you find out?"

"My mother was a teacher… I would visit her every morning or evening, depending on the lesson. Growing up, I felt I was destined to fight for Olympus. So much that I began preparing for my combat training at age 12."

"12!? I didn't even get to drive 'til I was 17!"

"One day, when I was 15… I suppose my ambitions have become too great. That was when she told me to never forget who I am deep down, recognize that all life, no matter how big or small, is precious… She told me that as much as I can strive to fight with the gods, I must never lose touch with my humanity… And that was when I figured it out.”

Hestius proceeds to recall this moment in time, when the bond between a mother and his son was shattered. The dark violet-haired woman drifts about in her cabin, as the young demigod sits with his attention focused on her, while the fireplace illuminates the premises.

“You have shown tremendous progress since we began, Hestius.” Gabriella smiles at the young warrior. “Everything about the Earth and heavens I have taught you has led to this very moment.” Slowly, she sits by him. “Watching you grow has been one of the greatest honors I have experienced.”

The redhead, at ease, smiles back to her. “Thank you, Gabriella. I will not let your teachings go to waste. They have proven to be very valuable to me, and they shall remain so on the field of battle when I am away.”

“I would certainly hope so.” she laughs. “But our lessons have yet to be concluded, young one.”

“What is there left to learn?” Hestius raises a brow.

Gabriella looks out to the window, gazing at the stars and night sky– all before sulking ever so slightly. “I know not when we will meet again… But I suppose I will teach you the most important lesson for last.”

Hestius looks slightly more confused, watching her.

Gabriella looks back to the demigod. "Hestius… You have expressed great knowledge and wisdom. With your passion to become a soldier, I have no doubt in my heart and soul that you will grow to become a great man. I had even stressed the importance of the very value that all living things hold in this world… and that includes you, my son." Gabriella leans over to caress the young warrior's cheek. "Promise me that when you are out there, you not only remember everything I have taught you, nor everyone who has supported you along the way… promise me that you will never forget who you are. To fight amongst gods, you must become one– but even so, never stray away from who you are deep down at heart."

Hestius stares into the eyes of his teacher. "... Y-Your… son?"

Gabriella lets out a soft gasp, realizing what she has done.

"What do you mean by this?" the demigod's voice raises. "Why did you call me that?"

"G-Gab– H-Hestius, please…" the woman cowers.

"To fight amongst gods, I must become one…? What are you suggesting? I am an immortal through and through, am I not? Hephaestus is my father, and Aphrodite is my mother– there is no other way around it."

Gabriella sits still as guilt begins to shroud over her entire being. "I…" Tears slowly start to tremble from her eyes. "I am sorry, Hestius…"

The demigod's eyes widened. "After all these years… you have lied to me…?" his body begins to shake. "I am… not a god?"

"Please, listen…" The tears flow down her face.

"That means they lied to me, too…" Hestius clenches his hands into fists as his blood begins to boil. "How could all of you have hid this from me!?"

"I-It was for your own good, I swear!"

"My own good!? What is so good about living through an entire falsehood!?"

"Hear me, Hestius." Gabriella sniffles. "Please understand, it was the only way to keep you safe–"

"Safe from what!?"

"Let me finish! We did not want you to be an outcast. We feared that terrible things would have happened to you if the other gods had found out!"

"To me? Are you sure it was not some scheme to cover for you and my father?"

"It is not like that! Look at it this way: your achievements are unlike any other mortal. You truly have the blood of a god, but the fact that you are also human makes you even more special."

"Special…? I am but a freak."

"No son of mine is a freak of any sort… Please, Gabriel… Surely you can imagine the pain of having to keep this from you, for this was the only way I could raise you as a mother."

The demigod watches her, tears also form their roots in his face. "Gabriel… Is that my real name?"

Gabriella nods carefully.

Time stands still between them.

"Well…" he utters. "They say knowledge is power. Power can be a curse... It all comes full circle."

The woman sinks her head.

"... I suppose there is nothing left here… Like you said, it is unknown whether our paths will cross again. As much as I had appreciated the many years of our time together, it seems I must bid you farewell."

The young warrior, with anger and hatred in his heart, leaves the cabin, and makes his way back to Olympus. Meanwhile, Gabriella is a broken, uncontrollable mess of tears.

"I am sorry, beloved... Please look after our son."

As fire lights their campsite, Andy watches the demigod through this recollection.

"And how did that go...?" he asks.

"... I never saw her again."

Andy tenses.

"I was cruel to her when she told me everything... I cursed her for keeping this from me my whole life at that moment. But I suppose, in some sort of twisted irony, that I had only cursed myself for condemning my own humanity... I could hardly stand it, then. Even when my father explained it all to me."

"Damn... That's rough, dude...."

Hestius nods. "I have come to realize he took no pleasure in hiding this from me. Same for my mother, and Aphrodite. It was all on me, for the path I chose was what led to this. Though, I imagine it would not be so different if it were any other way."

"Well... No one said life was fair. Sometimes, you just gotta pick whatever would hurt the least."

"I am certain my parents felt the same... Now all that remains of them is Titanious."

The two young men sit quietly for a moment before Andy speaks to him again.

"So you said Hestius was a name that was given to you to hide your humanity… Is that not your real name?"

The demigod clenches his skewer a bit tighter. "…My real name is Gabriel… Given to me by my father, and after my mother."

"And you mother?"

"… Gabriella." he wipes his face.

"What about Aphrodite? I'm sure she went through the ringer with it, too, right?"

"I only distanced myself from her. But the fact of the matter is… if I had one chance to tell my mother that I acknowledge the rashness of my actions, that I am sorry, and to thank her for what she had done for me, I would… Same for my father, and Aphrodite, too."

Slowly, tears begin to form alongside the redhead's eyes. Andy chimes in.

"You know, what? I think your parents know how you feel…"

"Is that so?"

"Well… My real dad died before I was born. I never got to know him. But, what I do know is that he watches over me." Andy gestures to the clouds. "Don't see a reason for him not to."

"My condolences, Andy."

"It's all good." He looks back at his friend. "In the end, I'm just glad I have people who have my back no matter what. And you did, too! You just… didn't know how to handle it, and it was just an unfortunate situation."

The demigod continues to stare at the fire, as the tears proceed to treat lightly down his face.

"Look… I know how hard it is, man. They say life's a game, and it all depends on how we play the hand we're dealt. But, even if you think you made a bad play, you still have your deck. And while you think you only have Titanious, you found a new family here on Earth. I mean, you're almost like the cool big brother I never had, if I'm being honest. And Hades? Well, who knows what old Skeletor is up to, but I'm sure he admires you enough. Like, we wouldn't even be here if it weren't for him."

The redhead gently swipes the blunt side of his thumb around his eyes. "You are correct… As much as it pains me that they are no longer here, I have never been more thankful for my parents looking back. And the same goes for you, and Hades as well…" he looks to the man he can truly consider his friend "Thank you, Andy. For not only being a great ally, but for helping me through these times."

"It's no problem." He pauses. "By the way, Gabriel's not a bad name. Sounds more… real, and genuine, I'd say. It's your mom's name, after all."

The demigod smiles gently. "Indeed it is… And you are free to call me that."

"Sounds good! And just one more thing, if you don't mind…"

Gabriel faces Andy with curiosity.

"... You got any war stories?"

"Oh, plenty!" He laughs. "Here, get me one of those… what do you call them?"

"A marshmallow? Right away!"

The two men, Andy and Gabriel, continue their night around the campfire– relishing in the sugary goodness of s'mores, and the tenderness of the occasional meat skewer, as the demigod tells stories of the war on Olympus, and the many victories he and Zeus' army had endured. Tales where Titanious battled valiantly against the forces of Ares. All until Andy finds himself passed out after having to heat Gabriel's constant blabbering, despite being the one who asked.

2,500 years ago on Olympus, Hephaestus is in his armory, hammering away at molten cratonium, crafting a bladed weapon. Gabriel enters, making way to his chambers.

"You are home quite early, Hestius!" calls the fire god.

The demigod stops in his tracks. "You mean Gabriel?"

Hephaestus is stunned, and swiftly looks over to him. "What do you mean?"

"Gabriella told me everything." He turns toward his father. "That I am a mere half-breed, and that you two and Aphrodite tried to cover it up."

Pausing, something collapses in the god's heart, as if a temple has crumbled within him. "Surely you understand why, yes?"

"What I do not understand is how a god like yourself could allow me to be born."

"That is enough."

"Were you so pitiful over Aphrodite choosing Ares over you that you decided to mate with a vulnerable human instead?"

"Silence!" Hephaestus shouts before storming in his son's direction, quickly pulling him by the shoulders. "Do not ever talk about your mother in such a manner!"

"Or what, you will disown me? Only adding to the mistakes you have brought upon yourself?"

"You are NOT a mistake, boy! The only mistake I have made was keeping this from you your whole life, and I acknowledge that, deeply."

"So why even lie? I could not simply live a normal life?"

"Son, you *are* normal. We have done everything to make sure of that!"

Gabriel watches his father, whose face goes from something rageful, slowly forming into something sad.

"There was no question in my mind that you would have found out eventually… But know that what your mother and I had was truer than what you could imagine. We *wanted* to have you as our son. We wanted someone who could possess the strengths of both a god and a mortal man. Even more so than the mighty Hercules. And you, Gabriel, are that icon– the icon that the people of Earth and Olympus can strive to become."

The demigod lowers his head slightly.

"But in time, you will become something greater… Come."

Hephaestus releases his son from his clutches, and the two of them exit their home, and wander through Olympus.

The fire god takes Gabriel to the grounds where they will celebrate his graduation ceremony, and leads him around the stage, and behind a large curtain.

Hephaestus enters the rear of the event. "I would hate to ruin the surprise, but you are an eager one after all."

Gabriel follows behind, and comes to a stop. Before his eyes, a colossal humanoid machine, covered in crimson, and accents of gold, standing 60 meters tall.

"What is this?" asks the demigod.

"This is Titanious. My life's work, and my gift to you."

"What does it do?"

"It will allow you to reach your full potential. You may not be a god, but with Titanious, you are no different. With its might, your heart, and everything your mother has taught, you will become an unstoppable force of not only Olympus, but Earth as well. But to become a god or a demon will be your choice, Gabriel. What you see is the very legacy of myself and Gabriella."

Gabriel gazes upon the deep purple eyes of the giant mech, who looks as if it is standing victoriously, ready to fight.

Back to now, as the young man in glasses lies in his tent, Gabriel marches off. The demigod uses the moonlight above him as a guide to find a gorgeous view of Greece and the night sky above. Eventually, he finds himself standing near the edge of a stone cliff, and looks off into the distance.

"Father... mother... Aphrodite... Zeus... Hades... Andy... Thank you for everything... And Ares... I am coming for you."

While the conflict between two worlds may be at ease for now, this is not the time to rest. The power of Ares still lurks within the depths of Tartarus, growing, becoming even more ready to conquer the Earth. But fret not, for the fateful reunion between the son of Hephaestus and the god of war will come. And when that time arrives, it will be for the ages. A feud, which had run for entire millennia, will come to an end. The battle for the fate of the world draws near, and let it be known that as long as good exists in this world, evil will tremble before it– for righteousness shall prevail, like a burning star soaring through the heavens.

To be continued in

TITANIOUS

BOOK TWO : HEAVENLY FIRE ANGEL

Coming 2025

Davis Madole grew up in Allen, TX as a student athlete in football and wrestling. Over the years, he immersed himself with an ever growing interest in science fiction, being raised on movies like *The Iron Giant*, *Transformers*, and the *Godzilla* series. He would even expose himself to the wonderful world of anime, getting into shows like *Urusei Yatsura*, *Fist of the North Star*, and *Mobile Suit Gundam*. These are the things that would inspire Davis to start his YouTube channel "TitanGoji!,"

where he would discuss and analyze various aspects of Japanese media and anything adjacent, from *Ultraman* to *Attack on Titan*, in the form of video essays. With a desire to create, Davis would go on to study film and writing at Austin College in Sherman, TX, where he would not only produce his own movies, but also graduate in 2022 with bachelor of arts degrees in media studies and creative writing. Additionally, he would pick up coaching in the fields of personal training, and strength and conditioning through the International Sports Science Association to support his hobbies and passion in producing content through various forms, and to honor the legacy of his family name, and his late parents who have inspired him to take on these paths.

You can find Davis on YouTube, Instagram, and Twitter @titangoji.

For more updates on the TITANIOUS series, follow @TeamTitanious on Twitter.